OXFORD WORLD'S CLASSICS

THE DIARY OF A NOBODY

GEORGE GROSSMITH (1847–1912), worked as a police-court reporter before embarking on a career as a singer and comedian in 1870. From 1877 to 1889 he was a prominent member of the D'Oyly Carte Company and played many leading roles in Gilbert and Sullivan operas. Subsequently, he toured Great Britain and the United States as a singer and entertainer until 1901. Apart from works of reminiscence, *The Diary of a Nobody* (1892) is his only book-length publication.

WEEDON GROSSMITH (1854–1919), George's brother, trained as an artist at the West London School of Art and the Royal Academy. He was not financially successful as a painter, however, and from 1885 also pursued a career on the stage. He published one novel, *A Woman with a History* (1896), and a number of plays, including *The Night of the Party* (1901). Weedon became manager of Terry's Theatre, London, and continued to act there and elsewhere until 1917.

KATE FLINT is Professor of English at Rutgers University. She is author of *The Woman Reader 1837–1914* (1993), and of numerous articles on nineteenth- and twentieth-century fiction and cultural history.

OXFORD WORLD'S CLASSICS

*For over 100 years Oxford World's Classics have brought
readers closer to the world's great literature. Now with over 700
titles—from the 4,000-year-old myths of Mesopotamia to the
twentieth century's greatest novels—the series makes available
lesser-known as well as celebrated writing.*

*The pocket-sized hardbacks of the early years contained
introductions by Virginia Woolf, T. S. Eliot, Graham Greene,
and other literary figures which enriched the experience of reading.
Today the series is recognized for its fine scholarship and
reliability in texts that span world literature, drama and poetry,
religion, philosophy and politics. Each edition includes perceptive
commentary and essential background information to meet the
changing needs of readers.*

OXFORD WORLD'S CLASSICS

GEORGE AND WEEDON GROSSMITH

The Diary of a Nobody

Edited with an Introduction and Notes by
KATE FLINT

OXFORD
UNIVERSITY PRESS

OXFORD

UNIVERSITY PRESS

Great Clarendon Street, Oxford OX2 6DP

Oxford University Press is a department of the University of Oxford.
It furthers the University's objective of excellence in research, scholarship,
and education by publishing worldwide in

Oxford New York

Athens Auckland Bangkok Bogotá Buenos Aires Calcutta
Cape Town Chennai Dar es Salaam Delhi Florence Hong Kong Istanbul
Karachi Kuala Lumpur Madrid Melbourne Mexico City Mumbai
Nairobi Paris São Paulo Singapore Taipei Tokyo Toronto Warsaw

with associated companies in Berlin Ibadan

Oxford is a registered trade mark of Oxford University Press
in the UK and in certain other countries

Published in the United States
by Oxford University Press Inc., New York

First published as an Oxford paperback 1995
Reissued as an Oxford World's Classics paperback 1998
Reissued 2008

British Library Cataloguing in Publication Data

Data available

Library of Congress Cataloging in Publication Data

Data available

ISB 978–0–19–954015–0

8

Printed and bound in Great Britain by Clays Ltd, Elcograf S.p.A.

CONTENTS

Introduction   vii

Note on the Text   xxiv

Select Bibliography   xxvi

A Chronology of George and Weedon Grossmith   xxix

THE DIARY OF A NOBODY   1

Explanatory Notes   137

INTRODUCTION

George and Weedon Grossmith's *The Diary of a Nobody* is a cultural icon. It has long been synonymous with a type of Englishness. Hilaire Belloc hyperbolically called it 'a book which is one of the half-dozen immortal achievements of our time . . . a glory for us all';[1] John Betjeman described it as an 'immortal book'.[2] The anxious, preposterous self-importance of the book's anti-hero, Charles Pooter, has stamped his name on the English language to create an affectionately derogatory adjective: 'a Pooterish little man'; 'So many square miles of vapid and banal and Pooterish suburb.'[3] Pooter's attitudes are the epitome of what David Thorns has located as the central myth of suburbia's identity: 'the centre of the middlebrow, conformist, respectable uninspiring members of society who are quite content to potter around in their own rather limited world.'[4] This is a world which simultaneously inspires affection for its safe familiarity, and a desire to rise up against its imaginative limitations and its conservative complacency. One of the strengths of *The Diary of a Nobody* is that it is at one and the same time a celebration and a gentle critique.

The Diary of a Nobody was initially published in *Punch*. The first instalment appeared on 26 May 1888, and the *Diary* featured in twelve of the next sixteen issues, between June and September. It then broke off for two months, a fact which explains the introduction of what otherwise seems, for a while, a melodramatic conspiracy against Pooter's chroniclings. He explodes, on the fictional 30 October: 'I should very much like to know who has wilfully torn the last five or six weeks out of my diary. It is perfectly monstrous!' (p. 50). This entry, published on 17 November 1888, heralded the second run of the *Diary*, which last appeared on 11 May 1889 with

[1] Hilaire Belloc, 'On People in Books', quoted in George Grossmith and Weedon Grossmith, *The Diary of a Nobody*, with a Memoir of the two brothers by B. W. Findon (J. W. Arrowsmith, Bristol, 5th edn. 1920), 21.

[2] Quoted in Bevis Hillier, *Young Betjeman* (John Murray, 1988), 63.

[3] *New Statesman* (11 Mar. 1966), 349; *Times Literary Supplement* (24 Feb. 1978), 229: both cited in the *Oxford English Dictionary*, 2nd edn.

[4] David Thorns, *Suburbia* (1972; Paladin, 1973), 149.

the entry for 21 March. 'Today I shall conclude my diary, for it is one of the happiest days of my life', Pooter proudly writes, before recording how his employer, Mr Perkupp, has at last taken on his troublesome son Lupin. The genealogy of tedium seems assured: 'My boy in the same office as myself—we can go down together by the bus, come home together, and who knows but in the course of time he may take a great interest in our little home' (p. 98), even if the chapters added when the book was published in volume form, during the summer of 1892, quickly demolish this hope.

Frank Burnand, the editor of *Punch* since 1880, had for some time been a friend of the Grossmith brothers.[5] George Grossmith (1847–1912), or 'Gee Gee' as he styled himself, had already published in its pages a short sketch, 'The Society Dramatist' (Apr. 1883), and ten skits of police court life, 'Very Trying: a record of a few trials of patience', in 1884. Whilst still at school, George Grossmith had begun to act as a deputy for his father, a police-court reporter, at Bow Street, and between 1866 and 1869 this provided his main income. His attempt to read for the bar came to nothing. From boyhood, however, he had entertained friends by singing comic songs to his own piano accompaniment, and from 1864 he began to give performances at 'penny readings' of songs and sketches of contemporary life, most of which he wrote himself. In 1870 he was engaged by John Henry Pepper to perform in his entertainment at the Polytechnic, Regent Street, and similar engagements followed: until 1876 he toured variety theatres, sometimes with his father, sometimes with Mrs Howard Paul or with Florence Marryat, sometimes alone. In 1877 he was engaged by Richard D'Oyly to take the part of John Wellington Wells in Gilbert and Sullivan's *The Sorcerer*, and for the next twelve years was a regular Gilbert and Sullivan performer—playing Reginald Bunthorne in *Patience*, the Lord Chancellor in *Iolanthe*, King Gama in *Princess Ida*, and Ko-Ko in *The Mikado* among other roles, excelling in the rapid enunciations of patter-songs. It was in his D'Oyly Carte capacity that he appeared

[5] For biographical details of the Grossmith brothers, see, (in addition to the *Dictionary of National Biography*) Tony Joseph, *George Grossmith: Biography of a Savoyard* (T. Joseph, Bristol, 1982) and their own autobiographies: George Grossmith, *A Society Clown* (J. W. Arrowsmith, Bristol, 1888) and *Piano and I* (J. W. Arrowsmith, Bristol, 1910), and Weedon Grossmith, *From Studio to Stage* (John Lane, 1913).

in—more-or-less—his own likeness in *Punch*, as 'the aesthetic Bunthorne, the greenery yallery, Grosvenor Gallery, young man'; as 'The Performing Gee-Gee' (as King Gama) and, in an even more pointed play on his name, in 'Carte and Gee-Gee', a cartoon showing a horse with George's head pulling a cart on which rode Richard D'Oyly Carte. This strong interest in theatricality comes across well in the *Diary*, whether in the trip with the Jameses to see *Brown Bushes* at the Tank Theatre, Islington, or in Lupin's enthusiasm for, and involvement with, the Holloway Comedians, or Mr Burwin-Fosselton's impersonation of Henry Irving. Something of an in-joke between the two brothers seems to be going on here: 'Mr Henry Irving and his Leetle Dog' was a frequent item in George's repertoire before his Gilbert and Sullivan days, and Weedon also performed his own Irving imitation for private amusement. He acted alongside Irving himself in May 1888. George resigned from the D'Oyly Carte company in 1889, and resumed a highly successful solo performance career, touring almost continually. His recital-entertainment shows were high earners: he could take as much as £380 at the Free Hall, Manchester, one evening, and then £430 the next afternoon at the Philharmonic, Liverpool.

Weedon's (1854–1919) career differed from George's in that before going on the stage he trained and practised as an artist, studying first at the West London School of Art and then at the Royal Academy. He exhibited regularly at the Royal Academy and at the new, fashionable Grosvenor Gallery, but had difficulty making a living as a painter, so turned to an alternative career as a successful comic actor. He excelled, as the *Dictionary of National Biography* entry by Harold Child puts it, in playing 'small, underbred, unhappy men'. He also accepted commissions as an illustrator; wrote for *Punch* and the *Art Journal*, and brought out a novel in his own right, *A Woman with a History* (1896). The extent of his collaboration on *The Diary of a Nobody* is unclear, however. All the *Punch* payments were made to George alone, suggesting—although not proving—his single-handed responsibility for the text. The first episodes were not illustrated; only from 24 November 1888 was the *Diary* accompanied by thumbnail sketches. But these were not Weedon's drawings, nor did they bear any relevance to the text they accompanied—rather, they were fillers, in house style, such as

'Nobody Nose' (1 Dec. 1888, p. 256), depicting a head with a large Mr Punch nose, on stick legs, with stick arms holding a volume inscribed 'My Diary'.

The illustrations became an integral part of *The Diary of a Nobody* when the Grossmiths published it in book form. With the exception of the seven additional chapters, few other important alterations were made. Those that appear seem largely padding which emphasizes Pooter's lack of ability to laugh at his own self-importance, his own absurdity, except when it can be turned into an opportunity for a laborious pun: his attempt to match the colour of the stair paint, which turns into a mini-saga of mismatching colours; the episode when his clip-on black bow tie falls into the theatre pit; the latter section of the Mansion House party ('Before I could think of a reply . . .)' (p. 28) to the end of the chapter; the paragraphs extolling the happiness of the Pooters' married life (p. 65), and the running story of the failure of the *Blackfriars Bi-weekly News* to print the Pooters' names correctly. There was probably something of the autobiographical in this last incident: 'People never get the name of Grossmith right. About August 12th it'll be Grousesmith; September 29th, Goosesmith; Christmas, Ghostsmith; and the last day of the old year, Grogsmith.'[6] Pooter himself was to suffer from misrepresentation again a couple of years later, when Marion Spielmann, in *The History of 'Punch'* (1895) described the *Diary*, in a supercilious and inaccurate manner, as 'a domestic record of considerable length, which dealt in an extremely earnest way with Mr. Samuel Porter, who lived in a small villa in Holloway, and had trouble with his drains, and was sometimes late at the office . . .'.[7]

Further changes which took place before volume publication are tiny in themselves, but testify to the Grossmiths' commitment to contemporaneity and to picking precisely the right cultural signifiers. Titles of popular songs are brought right up to date and fitted to their performers: 'Maggie's Secret' and 'Why don't the men propose?', sung by Mrs Cummings, become 'No, Sir' and the enduringly popular 'The Garden of Sleep' (p. 34), whilst Lupin's girlfriend

[6] Quoted Joseph, *George Grossmith*, 169.
[7] M. H. Spielmann, *The History of 'Punch'* (Cassell and Co., 1895), 392.

Lily attempts 'Some Day' (p. 61) rather than the melancholy 'The Garden of Sleep'. More intriguing is the addition to the sideboard for the 14 November party of 'a Paysandu tongue': clearly a bought item designed to impress, but also signifying quintessential Englishness. Holly, the resolutely homeloving, xenophobic narrator of Rider Haggard's *She* (1887), gains comfort from opening one of these tinned tongues—specified by name—when the going gets rough in Africa; *The Complete Indian Housekeeper and Cook* (1890) tells expatriots that 'The best tinned meat is a Paysandu ox tongue'.[8]

The Diary of a Nobody was, indeed, very much of its moment. The *Oxford English Dictionary* credits it with over twenty neologisms, from Lupin's expression ' "I've got the chuck!" ' to 'bread-pills' (as in domestic missiles which get chucked), 'dead-cert', and 'a good address'. Carrie Pooter tries to follow mildly avant-garde current fashions in interior decoration (more convincingly than her husband's wild wieldings of brushfuls of red paint in the direction of the servant's bedroom and even the bath): she ties Liberty bows at the four corners of their enlarged and tinted photographs, and follows her friend Mrs James's lead in writing on dark slate-coloured paper with white ink, and in draping the mantelpiece and putting little toy spiders, frogs, and beetles all over it.

Spiritualism—which features importantly in Chapter XXII—had a strong revival as a craze in the 1880s when, as Alex Owen points out, there was 'a regrouping of the forces of spiritualist respectability in the face of attack and ridicule, and a closing down of any discussion that could be construed as favouring the licentious or immoral. The ideology of home and family, representing social stability, decency, and morality, prevailed in the spiritualist camp.'[9] Again, the *Diary* here functions as a vehicle for a private joke: Florence Singleyet's *There is no Birth*, in which Carrie is immersed on 30 May, is a flimsy disguise for *There is no Death* (1891), published by George's former theatrical touring companion, Florence Marryat. In *A Society Clown* he records how he once took part in a table-rapping session with Marryat, and was berated by her for his

---

[8] Two Twenty Years' Residents [Flora Annie Steele and Grace Gardiner], *The Complete Indian Housekeeper and Cook* (Edinburgh: Frank Murray, 1890), 181.

[9] Alex Owen, *The Darkened Room. Women, Power and Spiritualism in Late Victorian England* (Virago Press, 1989), 38–9.

sceptical disrespect.[10] Further topicality is provided by the Pooters' discussion 'about the letters on "Is Marriage a Failure?"' predictably coming to the smug conclusion 'It has been no failure in our case' (p. 51). These letters appeared in the *Daily Telegraph* during the summer of 1888, prompting *Punch* to print half a page of spoof letters on the same subject and to answer the question posed with the comment 'Evidently not, as it contrives to fill two or three columns every day, and keeps up the circulation of the *D.T.* in the D.S., or Dull Season' (25 Aug. 1888, p. 87).

T. W. H. Crosland, in *The Suburbans* (1905), commented that 'It is a singular but nevertheless instructive fact that we owe pretty well the whole of the morbid movements and discussions of the past half-century to the delicate genius of Suburbia. Women's rights were first broached, and bloomers first worn, in Suburbia. "Is marriage a failure?" was an exceedingly bitter cry out of the sick married soul of Suburbia.'[11] Crosland was fascinated by the suburb, but had little sympathy with it or its 'pitiful people! Of its dead-level of dulness and weariness and meanness and hard-upness who shall relieve it?'[12] 'In Suburbia', he notes scathingly, 'we must, above all things, be consistently and undeviatingly and abidingly respectable':[13] a remark reflecting the Pooters' anxiety about keeping up appearances, about having calling-cards to leave, about the use of slang, about how far one might go even within the privacy of one's home. ('"Consequences" again this evening. Not quite so successful as last night; Gowing having several times overstepped the limits of good taste' (p. 34).) If the 'suburbans' have a philosophy, Crosland remarks, it is the attitude of small-minded conservatism, that 'whatever is, is best': 'It is this assumption that has induced in the bosoms of the suburbans a sublime appreciation of red-brick villas, seven-guinea saddle-bag suites, ceraceous fruit in glass shades, pampas grass, hire-system gramophones, anecdotal oleographs . . .'[14] and, one might add, looking around the Pooter home, pretty blue-wool mats to stand vases on, and 'a pair of stags' heads made of plaster-of-Paris and coloured brown. They will look just the thing for our little hall, and give it style' (p. 47). In the embellishment of their home, sedulously aping

[10] George Grossmith, *A Society Clown*, 86.

[11] T. W. H. Crosland, *The Suburbans* (John Lane, 1905), 69.

[12] Ibid. 24.   [13] Ibid. 17.   [14] Ibid. 35.

the decor of those who come from a far more leisured class, the Pooters are classic victims of what Thorstein Veblen, observing late-nineteenth-century society, called 'conspicuous consumption', the display of possessions chiefly remarkable for their lack of serviceability, except to signify aspiration, in a vague sense, and 'reputability': 'the taste to which these effects of household adornment and tidiness appeal is a taste which has been formed under the selective guidance of a canon of propriety that demands just these evidences of wasted effort.'[15] The same aspirational tendencies are seen in other leisure pursuits, markers of having achieved a certain income level. This is most obvious in the taking of the annual summer holiday in a seaside boarding house which, if hardly glamorous, provides a focus to the year, an excuse to buy new clothes, to play games and let off steam.[16]

The Pooters' world is precisely that described by C. F. G. Masterman, slightly more sympathetically than Crosland, in *The Condition of England* (1909):

It is a life of Security; a life of Sedentary occupation; a life of Respectability; and these three qualities give the key to its special characteristics. Its male population is engaged in all its working hours in small, crowded offices, under artificial light, doing immense sums, adding up other men's accounts, writing other men's letters. It is sucked into the City at daybreak, and scattered again as darkness falls. It finds itself towards evening in its own territory in the miles and miles of little red houses in little silent streets, in number defying imagination. Each boasts its pleasant drawing-room, its bow-window, its little front garden, its high-sounding title—'Acacia Villa', or 'Camperdown Lodge'—attesting unconquered human aspiration. There are many interests beyond the working hours: here a greenhouse filled with chrysanthemums, a bicycle shed, a tennis lawn. The women, with their single domestic servants, now so difficult to get, and so exacting when found, find time hang rather heavy on their hands. But there are excursions to shopping centres in the West End, and pious sociabilities, and occasional theatre visits, and the interests of home.[17]

[15] Thorstein Veblen, *The Theory of the Leisure Class: An Economic Study in the Evolution of Institutions* (Macmillan, 1899), 83.

[16] For the growth in seaside holidays, see John Urry, 'Mass Tourism and the Rise and Fall of the Seaside Resort', ch. 2 of *The Tourist Gaze: Leisure and Travel in Contemporary Societies* (Sage Publications, 1990), 16–39; J. Walton, *The English Seaside Resort: A Social History, 1750–1914* (Leicester University Press, 1983); and James Walvin, *Beside the Seaside* (Allen Lane, 1978).

[17] C. F. G. Masterman, *The Condition of England* (Methuen & Co., 1909), 70.

Throughout the nineteenth century, the London suburbs had been spreading relentlessly. In his invaluable, detailed study of the growth of one particular suburb, Camberwell, H. J. Dyos records how between 1802 and 1898 the population of this location grew from 7,059 to 253,076; that of Lewisham from 4,007 to 104,521. He claims that this expansion was most marked from the 1860s onwards, estimating that 'the outer ring of suburbs of Greater London . . . grew by about 50 per cent in each of the three intercensal periods between 1861 and 1891 and by 45 per cent in the decade 1891–1901'.[18] Yet as early as 1829 George Cruikshank produced a cartoon showing the departure of trees and hayricks and farm animals under a hail of bricks which spewed out of kilns; a retreat from advancing armies of chimney pots, from dense belching smoke, from the regimental ranks of scaffolding which propped up houses under construction, their outer walls already cracking. Dickens described this urban expansion in *Dombey and Son* (1848), where the 'frowzy fields, and cowhouses, and dunghills' of Camden Town mutate into 'villas, gardens, churches, healthy public walks' in the space of six years.[19] Wemmick, in *Great Expectations* (1861) is the prototype of the suburban resident Pooter is to become, literally raising and lowering the drawbridge of his Walworth residence (Pooter lets us know in his very first entry that 'there is a flight of ten steps up to the front door, which, by-the-by, we keep locked with the chain up' (p. 3)). This is the segregation of work and leisure of which Raymond Williams wrote in *Culture and Society* (1958), 'the suburban separation of "work" and "life" which has been the most common response of all to the difficulties of industrialism'.[20] It was recorded affectionately in verse by Ernest Radford in 1906:

[18] H. J. Dyos, *Victorian Suburb* (Leicester University Press, 1961), 19–20. For the growth of London suburbs, see further Helena Barrett and John Phillips, *Suburban Style: The British Home, 1840–1960* (Macdonald, 1987); Alan A. Jackson, *Semi-Detached London: Suburban Development, Life and Transport, 1900–39* (George Allen & Unwin, 1973); 'The Villa and the New Suburb', in Donald J. Olsen, *The Growth of Victorian London* (Batsford, 1976), 187–264; and F. M. L. Thompson (ed.), *The Rise of Suburbia* (Leicester University Press, 1982). Also relevant to the social history of the section of the population to which Charles Pooter belongs is Gregory Anderson, *Victorian Clerks* (Manchester University Press, 1976).

[19] Charles Dickens, *Dombey and Son* (1848; Harmondsworth: Penguin English Library, 1970), 121, 289.

[20] Raymond Williams, *Culture and Society* (1958; Harmondsworth: Penguin, 1961), 211.

He leaned upon the narrow wall
That set the limit to his ground,
And marvelled, thinking of it all,
That he such happiness had found.

He had no word for it but bliss;
He smoked his pipe; he thanked his stars;
And, what more wonderful than this?
He blessed the groaning, stinking cars

That made it doubly sweet to win
The respite of the hours apart
From all the broil and sin and din
Of London's damned money mart.[21]

The other side of the picture was to be given by George Orwell in
Coming Up for Air (1939), where the suburb is mocked as a 'line of
semi-detached torture-chambers where the poor little five-to-ten
pounders quake and shiver, every one of them with the boss twisting his tail and the wife riding him like a nightmare and the kids
sucking his blood like leeches'.[22] As F. M. L. Thompson puts it, in
neutral terms which allow for both idealization and contempt:
'The creation of an environment in which this division of middleclass male lives between a public world of work contacts and a
private world of family life was what the rise of suburbia was all
about.'[23]

Suburbia had its vociferous detractors. Condemnation of the trivi-
ality, the conventionality, the small-mindedness, the petty snobbery
of its inhabitants and of the crushing boredom of its lifestyle was
expressed by Crosland, by Walter Besant ('the life of a suburb without any society; no social gatherings or institutions; as dull a life as
mankind ever tolerated'[24]), by Masterman. As Cruikshank had done,
Masterman saw something apocalyptic in the spread of bricks and
mortar: 'North, East, South, and West the aggregation is silently
pushing outwards like some gigantic plasmodium: spreading slimy
arms over the surrounding fields, heavily dragging after them the

[21] Ernest Radford, 'Our Suburb', *A Collection of Poems* (Gibbings & Co., 1906), 60.
The 'cars' are the carriages of the underground railway.
[22] George Orwell, *Coming Up for Air* (Victor Gollancz, 1939), 17–18.
[23] F. M. L. Thompson, 'Introduction: The Rise of Suburbia', *Rise of Suburbia*, 9.
[24] Walter Besant, *London in the Nineteenth Century* (A. & C. Black, 1909), 262.

ruin of its desolation.'[25] The 61-year-old John Ruskin, whose views
on architecture fed their way into the Gothic elements of many a
suburban villa, mourned the passing of his childhood landscape.
Then, Croxted Lane was 'a green bye-road', separated by black-
berry hedges from the meadows each side, growing primroses, dai-
sies, purple thistles. Now, he claims, new forms of language are
necessary to describe 'the peculiar forces of devastation induced by
modern city life':

The fields each side of it are now mostly dug up for building, or cut
through into gaunt corners and nooks of blind ground by the wild cross-
ings and concurrencies of three railroads. Half a dozen handfuls of
new cottages, with Doric doors, are dropped here and there among
the gashed ground: the lane itself, now entirely grassless, is a deep-
rutted, heavy-hillocked cart-road, diverging gatelessly into various
brickfields or pieces of waste; and bordered on each side by heaps of—
Hades only knows what!—mixed dust of every unclean thing that can
crumble in drought, and mildew of every unclean thing that can rot or
rust in damp: ashes and rags, beer-bottles and old shoes, battered pans,
smashed crockery, shreds of nameless clothes, door-sweepings, floor-
sweepings, kitchen garbage, back-garden sewage, old iron, rotten timber
jagged with out-torn nails, cigar-ends, pipe-bowls, cinders, bones, and
ordure, indescribable; and, variously kneaded into, sticking to, or flutter-
ing foully here and there over all these, remnants, broadcast, of every
manner of newspaper, advertisement or big-lettered bill, festering and
flaunting out their last publicity in the pits of stinking dust and mortal
slime.[26]

Similar criticisms were to be found in the fiction of the late nineteenth and early twentieth centuries. Here again, the environment
itself is presented as being under assault. In George Egerton's short
story 'Wedlock' (1894), for example, 'a terrace of new jerrybuilt
houses in a genteel suburb' is being built on the remains of a grand
old garden:

[25] C. F. G. Masterman, 'The Burden of London', *In Peril of Change* (T. Fisher
Unwin, 1905), 165.
[26] John Ruskin, *Fiction, Fair and Foul* (1880–81), *The Works of John Ruskin*, ed. E. T.
Cook and Alexander Wedderburn, Library Edition, 39 vols. (George Allen, 1903–12)
xxxiv. 266–7. For Ruskin and suburbia, see Dinah Birch, 'A Life in Writing: Ruskin
and the Uses of Suburbia', in J. B. Bullen (ed.), *Writing and Victorianism* (Longman,
1997), 234–49.

a granite urn, portions of a deftly carven shield … lie in the trampled grass. The road in front is scarcely begun, and the smart butchers' carts sink into the soft mud and red brick-dust, broken glass, and shavings; yet many of the houses are occupied, and the unconquerable London soot has already made some of the cheap 'art' curtains look dingy … Victoria, Albert, and Alexandra figure in ornamental letters over the stained-glass latticed square of three pretentious houses, facing Gladstone, Cleopatra, and Lobelia.[27]

Above all, suburbia was condemned for its numbing effect on people's lives, for the cautious conformity that it engendered, for its self-protective social conservatism, for the boredom it produced. It comes under fire in the novels of George Gissing, of H. G. Wells, of E. M. Forster and George Orwell: indeed, it seems to change little between the Grossmiths' time and the Second World War, Orwell's description, in *Coming Up for Air*, reminding one that the nature of suburbia is stasis: 'The stucco front, the creosoted gate, the privet hedge, the green front door. The Laurels, the Myrtles, the Hawthorns, Mon Abris, Mon Repos, Belle Vue.'[28] Its association with reactionary forces has been noted by Roger Silverstone: 'Suburbia', he writes, 'has remained curiously invisible in the accounts of modernity. The suburban is seen, if at all and at best, as a consequence, an excrescence, a cancerous fungus, leaching the energy of the city, dependent and inert and ultimately self-destructive.'[29]

Yet alongside the condemnatory portrayals, fiction began to display a more sympathetic treatment of suburbia, and in many ways the Grossmiths' work is a forerunner of this.[30] Such writers as

---

[27] George Egerton, 'Wedlock' (1894; *Keynotes & Discords*, Virago Press, 1983), 115–16.

[28] Orwell, *Coming Up for Air*, 16.

[29] Roger Silverstone, 'Introduction', in Silverstone (ed.), *Visions of Suburbia* (Routledge, 1997), 4. This is a valuable revisionist collection of essays on the topic of suburbia.

[30] For fiction and suburbia, see Kate Flint, 'Fictional Suburbia', in Peter Humm, Paul Stigant, and Peter Widdowson (eds.), *Popular Fictions: Essays in Literature and History*, (Methuen, 1986), 111–26; Peter Keating, *The Haunted Study: A Social History of the English Novel 1875–1914* (Secker & Warburg, 1989), 319–27; and David Trotter, *The English Novel in History 1895–1920* (Routledge, 1993), 128–32. Keating (p. 320) makes the interesting point that 'The growing interest of early twentieth-century novelists in suburban life was in part a fairly straightforward recognition of a contemporary phenomenon, but it also embodied a determination to reverse the class bias of the slum novel, and, as the Labour Party became increasingly the official spokesman for

Keble Howard, Shan Bullock, and—in his later novels—William
Pett Ridge delineate the suburbs, and the lives of those who inhabit
them, with understanding, even idealism, rather than standing back
in a vantage point of implied superiority. The material culture of
this world—the displays of ferns, the stuffed birds, the mounted
photographs—may on occasion be lightly mocked, but it is a loving
mockery, based on the acceptance of the fact that characters, and
probably readers, are all engaged 'in making the best show we could.
The brass knocker, the bay window, the dining and drawing rooms,
establish the fact we had in view, the great suburban ideal of being
superior to the people next door.'[31] Suburbia may be stuffy, but it is
also safe, suggesting that domestic stability is achievable even in a
world of changing social values. Cicely, the New Woman novelist of
Pett Ridge's *A Clever Wife* (1895), returns thankfully to her husband's arms after her unsuccessful bid for independence, murmur-
ing, as they embrace on Clapham Common, '"I had no idea . . . I
had no idea that the suburbs could contain joy".'[32]

   The Grossmiths, however, are more subtle than much of the
suburban fiction that followed them in the way in which they acknowledge Pooter's vulnerability, and it is this vulnerability that in
many ways provides the essence of his lasting appeal, and offers a
point of tacit self-identification for some of his readers. Some of his
failings are instantly recognizable, like his utter reluctance to admit
to a hangover. However much Carrie might point out what he has
drunk the previous night, Pooter is always determined to blame
what he has eaten, or the 'unsettled weather' (p. 101). Some of his
weaknesses play on broader-based class fears, such as his concern
with etiquette and what is 'correct' at the level of manners. His
spontaneous gestures—seizing Carrie round the waist in order to
polka round the kitchen—rub up against his determination to find
the right wording in which to reply to a formal invitation. Pooter
would have been a natural target for the numerous little manuals
aimed at those with social aspirations in the nineteenth century, full
of such advice as

Masterman's "creature" of the abyss, to re-assert the right of the middle classes to
more sympathetic consideration.'

   [31] Shan Bullock, *Robert Thorne* (T. Werner Laurie, 1907), 249.
   [32] William Pett Ridge, *A Clever Wife* (R. Bentley & Son, 1895), 392.

Don't use slang. There is some slang that, according to Thackeray, is gentlemanly slang, and other slang that is vulgar. If one does not know the difference, let him avoid slang altogether, and then he will be safe . . . Don't beat a tattoo with your foot in company or anywhere, to the annoyance of others. Don't drum with your fingers on chair, table, or window-pane. Don't hum a tune. The instinct for making noises is a survival of savagery.[33]

One wonders what he would have made of further prohibitions in the same publication: 'Don't sneer at people, nor continually crack jokes at their expense . . . Don't make obvious puns. An occasional pun, if a good one, is a good thing; but a ceaseless flow of puns is simply maddening.'[34] This particular verbal habit was frequently remarked upon in these manuals as an area where caution was necessary: 'All kinds of wit, puns by no means excepted, give relish to social parties, when they spring up naturally and spontaneously out of the themes of conversation. But for a man to be constantly straining himself to make jokes is to render himself ridiculous, and to annoy the whole company, and is, therefore, what no gentleman will be guilty of.'[35] Pooter treads a fine line in this respect, as the Comings and Goings of his word-play on Cummings's and Gowing's names demonstrates.

Yet Pooter is not just vulnerable to the continual clash of his natural exuberance with the demand for respectability, but to broader forces of social change. His son, Lupin, does not, after all, meekly succeed him in the daily expedition to Mr Perkupp's firm for long, but wastes no time in seeing the old-fashioned, ultimately doomed way in which business is carried out there. Mr Perkupp and his team lack the cutthroat sharpness which will be necessary to succeed in the rapidly developing international financial markets. Lupin and 'Lillie Girl's' marriage—assuming the nuptials come off this time— will not produce, we may be sure, grandchildren with whom Charles and Carrie will be comfortable, but will spawn the future inhabitants of Evelyn Waugh's chrome-plated world of the moneyed and

---

[33] 'CENSOR', *Don't: A Manual of Mistakes and Improprieties more or less prevalent in Conduct and Speech* (Griffith & Farran, 1884), 50, 68.

[34] Ibid. 67, 36.

[35] *The Etiquette of Modern Society: A Guide to Good Manners in Every Possible Situation* (Ward, Lock & Co., 1883), 97.

stupid. Pooter may even come to be shocked by Carrie. He is mildly disconcerted, from time to time, by the influence the decidedly more avant-garde Mrs James has over her. Crosland, as we have seen, recognized that the suburbs were the natural breeding-ground for discussions concerning women's rights, and by 1909 (the year, incidentally, of Wells's *Ann Veronica*, which makes much the same point in fiction), Masterman was noting that in suburbia 'The women—or a remnant of them—are finding outlet for suppressed energy and proffered devotion in an agitation for the vote.'[36] Holloway will become better known for its gaol, in this respect, than for its suburban desirability.

But how desirable will Holloway continue to be, even for a conservative clerk? Pooter, of course, is enraptured by the reward Mr Perkupp gives him when (against the odds of Lupin's analysis of the business world) he introduces a wealthy American to the firm:

I find my eyes filling with tears as I pen the note of my interview this morning with Mr Perkupp. Addressing me, he said: 'My faithful servant, I will not dwell on the important service you have done our firm. You can never be sufficiently thanked. Let us change the subject. Do you like your house, and are you happy where you are?'

I replied: 'Yes, sir; I love my house and I love the neighbourhood, and could not bear to leave it.'

Mr Perkupp, to my surprise, said: 'Mr Pooter, I will purchase the freehold of that house, and present it to the most honest and most worthy man it has ever been my lot to meet.'

He shook my hand, and said he hoped my wife and I would be spared many years to enjoy it. (p. 135)

This episode—even mildly tempered with the news about Lupin's new engagement—provides a rounding-off to the *Diary*, turning it into a recognizable prototype for the suburban celebrations which were to follow at the hands of other authors. It is a confirmation of Pooter's love of home, a rooting of himself in his chosen suburb.

However, by the 1890s Holloway was barely suburb at all: it was on the verge of being thought of as city. It certainly did not approach the leafy status of that byword for early twentieth-century suburbia, Surbiton—as in Keble Howard's *The Smiths of Surbiton*

---

[36] Masterman, *Condition of England*, 84.

(1906). Pooter travels to work by bus—a form of transport which, Thompson notes, 'had a much more widespread effect than work-men's trains and fares in enabling the lower middle class and the artisans to push out into suburbia and to threaten the exclusiveness of middleclass suburbs'.[37] Yet the bus might not even have been strictly necessary for his journey to work: Alan Jackson classifies Holloway, along with Hackney and Islington, as a 'walking' settle-ment.[38] It is not a location which features in W. S. Clarke's compre-hensive guide of 1881 to 'those fair dwellings and picturesque retreats which form that lovely fringe—THE SUBURBAN HOMES OF LONDON!'—places such as Brixton and Clapham, Bromley and Bickley, Hendon, Mill Hill, and Cricklewood.[39] And, as Masterman points out, one generation's desirable residence, if it is situated too close to the centre of town, quickly becomes another generation's slum, 'as the original respectable emigrants move off again':

Contemplate Belle Vue or Fair Light estate some two or three years after completion ... The grotesque newness of the houses, the remains of the painted lines of mortar, the pretentious pillared porticoes and iron work in the front garden yield, like the remains of beauty in a withered face, a kind of half humorous, half pathetic touch to the prevailing decay. Cur-tains have disappeared from the front windows; the open doors disclose passages with blackened walls and staircases gaping with holes; unkempt children swarm in the streets; rubbish and waste paper line the gutters. The gin palace alone exhibits thriving vitality.[40]

The brick lobbed from next door might well be the portent of uncomfortable times ahead for 'The Laurels': even if the new neigh-bours do have friends who turn up in dog-carts, their rudeness and vulgarity is hard for Pooter to address.

The Diary of a Nobody is not a book which denies the existence of social change, nor, even, does it pretend that suburbia provides a model life-style which will necessarily be particularly successful in

[37] Thompson, *Rise of Suburbia*, 20.

[38] Jackson, *Semi-Detached London*, 22.

[39] [W. S. Clarke], *The Suburban Homes of London: A Residential Guide to Favourite London Localities, Their Society, Celebrities, and Associations with notes on their Rental, Rates, and House Accommodation* (Chatto and Windus, 1881), p. v.

[40] [C. F. G. Masterman], *From the Abyss: Of its Inhabitants by One of Them* (R. Brimley Johnson, 1902), 45–6.

resisting the less desirable aspects of the modern world. It is, none the less, a work which celebrates the ordinary, even while it demands that its readers laugh at taking quotidian minutiae too seriously. Its influence goes beyond the work of near-contemporary suburban novelists, however. Whilst the spoof diary was a genre already employed in the pages of *Punch*, the Grossmiths' particular brand of self-preoccupied seriousness was itself being imitated, or rather parodied, even whilst it was being published. *Punch's Almanack for 1889* (published with the 6 December 1888 *Punch*) contained 'Extracts from the Diary of a Dyspeptic':

January 1.—Another dreary weary year to be lived through! Oh, to be done with it all! Got as far as Club this afternoon. Walked home despairing of Humanity. Considerable pain in epigastrium. *Query—internal?*

February 14.—Pairing time. No one pairs with Me! My doom to drag through the melancholy days unloved, uncared-for, alone! Remember passage in some poet—forget whom and exact lines—but to effect that the entire animal creation, down to the very rabbits, had a mate, with the single exception of the poet himself. Pathetic idea, and my own case exactly. Fortunately, I hold *all* women in secret contempt. Too depressed for regular luncheon, but snatched a Bath bun and some ginger ale at Confectioner's. Wished I was dead several times on way home.[41]

It has certainly spawned more recent, if not always less laboured imitators, most notably Sue Townsend's painfully self-conscious, self-important, hapless Adrian Mole. In some ways, though, Pooter's true successors lie in situation comedies—in the BBC's *Terry and June, The Fall and Rise of Reginald Perrin, The Good Life, One Foot in the Grave*[42]—and in many of the playwright Alan Ayckbourn's suburban characters. Stuart E. Baker, analyzing the type of farce to be found in Ayckbourn's work, has written about it in perceptive terms which apply equally well to the *Diary*. Farce, as he distinguishes it from comedy, offers no promise of the renewal and reintegration of society: it demands that we laugh at life as we find it, 'condensing and heightening the dreadful facts that are the reality behind all farce. It paradoxically heightens the reality while dismiss-

---

[41] 'Extracts from the Diary of a Dyspeptic', *Punch's Almanack for 1889*, p. 8.

[42] For a discussion of the place of suburbia in situation comedies, films, and soap operas, see Andy Medhurst, 'Negotiating the Gnome Zone: Versions of Suburbia in British Popular Culture', Silverstone, *Visions of Suburbia*, 240–68.

ing it as a joke.' Ayckbourn's characters—like the Grossmiths'—are 'slow, silly, trivial, Philistine, pedestrian, petty, and utterly unexceptional except in their limitations. In real life such people are enormously uninteresting. Farce makes them interesting—or at least calls our attention to them—by placing them in extraordinary situations that allow the serious farceur to hold the mirror up to nature and show people "how badly you live, and how tiresome you are".'[43]

Pooter's limitations of vision are both part of the source of his appeal, and, ultimately, have the power to render him something of a victim. In the dream of the small man winning out which the Grossmiths present, they do, perhaps, call on a comic tradition which suggests that a reconciliatory spirit in some way animates the world, but the pattern of the book up to this point has not been to allow stability to persist for long. The diary form is, after all, a genre inimical to neat closure: the idea that he can finish with a flourish is, in fact, the final delusion in which Pooter persists. The idea that this man is one of themselves, but that readers can see what he does not, whilst still feeling benevolently sympathetic towards him—that they are, in some way, superior to their neighbour—provides the most enduring ground for the *Diary*'s popularity. The principles of suburbia are, after all, kept intact in the reading that it most readily invites.

[43] Stuart E. Baker, 'Ayckbourn and the Tradition of Farce', in Bernard F. Dukore (ed.), *Alan Ayckbourn: A Casebook* (Garland Publishing, 1991), 30, 36.

NOTE ON THE TEXT

The Diary of a Nobody was originally published in instalments in *Punch*, May 1888–May 1889.

26 May 1888	preamble, and 3–8 April
2 June 1888	9–12 April
9 June 1888	14–18 April
16 June 1888	19–23 April
23 June 1888	24–7 April
7 July 1888	28 April–3 May
14 July 1888	4–7 May
21 July 1888	8–9 May
28 July 1888	21 May–7 June
18 August 1888	30 July–3 August
25 August 1888	4–6 August
1 September 1888	11–20 August
15 September 1888	22–9 August
17 November 1888	30 October–3 November
24 November 1888	4–7 November
1 December 1888	8–13 November
15 December 1888	14 November
29 December 1888	15–18 November
19 January 1889	17–23 December
26 January 1889	24–8 December
2 February 1889	29–31 December
9 February 1889	1–5 January
2 March 1889	21–6 January
30 March 1889	8–12 February
4 May 1889	18–20 February
11 May 1889	20–1 March

Chapter XI and the final seven chapters were added when *The Diary of a Nobody* appeared in one volume in the summer of 1892, published by J. W. Arrowsmith, Bristol. The serial publication was by and large unillustrated, although it was occasionally accompanied by a thematically unrelated thumbnail sketch. Weedon Grossmith contributed the illustrations for the volume edition. The *Punch* payments were to George alone, suggesting that he was solely responsible for the text. For a discussion of the relatively few additions and alterations that were made, see the Introduction, pp. ix–xi. Many of these involved emphasizing Pooter's tendency towards a humourless self-importance, or updated topical references.

SELECT BIBLIOGRAPHY

General Background

Gregory Anderson, *Victorian Clerks* (Manchester: Manchester University Press, 1976).

Helena Barrett and John Phillips, *Suburban Style: The British Home, 1840–1960* (London: Macdonald, 1987).

Dinah Birch, 'A Life in Writing: Ruskin and the Uses of Suburbia', in J. B. Bullen (ed.), *Writing and Victorianism* (London: Longman, 1997), 234–49.

John Carey, *The Intellectuals and the Masses* (London: Faber, 1992).

[W. S. Clarke], *The Suburban Homes of London: A Residential Guide to Favourite London Localities* (London: William Spencer, 1881).

T. W. H. Crosland, *The Suburbans* (London: John Long, 1905).

H. J. Dyos, *Victorian Suburb* (Leicester: Leicester University Press, 1961).

——and D. Reeder, 'Slums and Suburbs' in H. J. Dyos and M. Wolff (eds.), *The Victorian City* (London: Routledge & Kegan Paul, 1973), 359–86.

Kate Flint, 'Fictional Suburbia', in Peter Humm, Paul Stigant, and Peter Widdowson (eds.), *Popular Fictions: Essays in Literature and History* (London: Methuen, 1986), 111–26.

George Grossmith, *A Society Clown* (Bristol: J. W. Arrowsmith, 1888).

——*Piano and I* (Bristol: J. W. Arrowsmith; London: Simpkin, Marshall, 1910).

Weedon Grossmith, *From Studio to Stage* (London: John Lane, 1913).

M. C. Hamard, 'Les Divertissements de la famille Pooter', *Cahiers Victoriens et Édouardiens*, 19 (1984), 11–21.

Tony Joseph, *George Grossmith: Biography of a Savoyard* (Bristol: Tony Joseph, 1982).

Peter Keating, *The Haunted Study; A Social History of the English Novel 1875–1914* (London: Secker and Warburg, 1989).

A. D. King, *Global Cities: Post-Imperialism and the Internationalisation of London* (London and New York: Routledge, 1990).

C. F. G. Masterman, *The Heart of the Empire* (London: T. Fisher Unwin, 1901).

[C. F. G. Masterman], *From the Abyss: Of its Inhabitants by One of Them* (London: R. B. Johnson, 1902).

——*In Peril of Change* (London: T. Fisher Unwin, 1905).

——*The Condition of England* (London: Methuen, 1909).

Paul Oliver, Ian David, and Ian Bentley, *Dunroamin: The Suburban Semi and its Enemies* (London: Barrie and Jenkins, 1981).

Donald J. Olsen, *The Growth of Victorian London* (London: Batsford, 1976).

Roy Porter, *London: A Social History* (London: Hamish Hamilton, 1994).

Roger Silverstone (ed.), *Visions of Suburbia* (London and New York: Routledge, 1997).

F. M. L. Thompson (ed.), *The Rise of Suburbia* (Leicester: Leicester University Press, 1982).

David C. Thorns, *Suburbia* (London: McGibbon & Kee), 1972.

David Trotter, *The English Novel in History 1895–1920* (London: Macmillan, 1993).

Thorstein Veblen, *The Theory of the Leisure Class: An Economic Study in the Evolution of Institutions* (London: 1899).

Novels set in, or with bearing on, suburbia

R. Andom [Alfred Walter Barrett], *Neighbours of Mine* (London: Stanley Paul & Co., 1912).

Alice and Claude Askew, *The Baxter Family* (London: F. V. White & Co., 1907).

Arnold Bennett, *A Man from the North* (London: John Lane, 1898).

J. D. Beresford, *The House in Demetrius Road* (London: William Heinemann, 1914).

Shan Bullock, *Robert Thorne* (London: T. Werner Laurie, 1907).

E. M. Forster, *Where Angels Fear to Tread* (London: Blackwoods, 1905).

—— *The Longest Journey* (London: Blackwoods, 1907).

—— *A Room with a View* (London: Edward Arnold, 1908).

George Gissing, *In the Year of Jubilee* (London: Lawrence & Bullen, 1894).

—— *The Whirlpool* (London: Lawrence & Bullen, 1894).

Keble Howard, *The Smiths of Surbiton* (London: Chapman and Hall, 1906).

Lucas Malet, *The Far Horizon* (London: Hutchinson, 1906).

Barry Pain, *Eliza* (London: S. H. Bousfield, 1900).

W. Carter Platts, *Timmins of Crickleton* (London: Digby, Long & Co, 1908).

Edwin Pugh, *A Street in Suburbia* (London: William Heinemann, 1895).

William Pett Ridge, *A Clever Wife* (London: R. Bentley & Son, 1895).

—— *Outside the Radius* (London: Hodder & Stoughton, 1895).

—— *69 Birnam Road* (London: Hodder & Stoughton, 1908).

—— *Nine to Six-Thirty* (London: Methuen, 1910).

John Collis Snaith, *William Jordan, Junior* (London: Archibald Constable, 1908).

Frank Swinnerton, *The Merry Heart* (London: Methuen, 1909).

H. G. Wells, *Tono-Bungay* (London: Macmillan, 1908).

——*Ann Veronica* (London: T. Fisher Unwin, 1909).

CHRONOLOGY

1847 George Grossmith born, c.9 December, to George Grossmith senior, a journalist and police-court reporter, who was also well known as a reciter and professional reader, and Louisa Emmeline Weedon Grossmith.

1854 Weedon Grossmith born 9 June.

1859 GG attends North London Collegiate School.

WG, after a short period at North London Collegiate and various small private schools, attends first the West London School of Art, and is subsequently admitted first as a probationer, then as a full student at the Royal Academy.

1864 GG begins to give performances as 'penny readings' of songs and sketches of contemporary life, mostly written by himself.

1865 GG begins to act as deputy for his father as a police-court reporter at Bow Street police court, whilst still attending school. This is his sole profession 1866–9. He starts to read for the bar, but this career never takes off.

1869 GG's burlesque *No Thoroughfare* staged.

1870 GG engaged by John Henry Pepper to perform in his entertainment at the Polytechnic, Regent Street. Other similar engagements follow: until 1877 he tours with his father, with Mrs Howard Paul, with Florence Marryat, and alone.

1873 GG marries Emmeline Rosa Noyce: they have two sons and two daughters. George Jr. (1874–1935) becomes an actor and entertainer, programme adviser to the BBC, and managing director of the Theatre Royal, Drury Lane; Lawrence (b. 1877) a comedy actor on stage and film, and portrait-painter; Ena (1896–1944) acts on stage and on film.

1877 GG is engaged by Richard D'Oyly Carte to take the part of John Wellington Wells in Gilbert and Sullivan's *The Sorcerer*. For the next twelve years, he is regularly employed in this series of operas. Roles include: Sir Joseph Porter (*H.M.S. Pinafore*), Major-General Stanley (*The Pirates of Penzance*), Reginald Bunthorne (*Patience*), the Lord Chancellor (*Iolanthe*), King Gama (*Princess Ida*), Ko-Ko (*The Mikado*), Robin Oakapple (*Ruddigore*), and Jack Point (*The Yeomen of the Guard*).

1879 WG's first major success as artist with three–quarter-length portrait of his father reading from *Pickwick*. He exhibits many times at the Royal Academy and the Grosvenor Gallery.

1880 24 April: GG senior dies of apoplexy.

1884 GG composes ten skits of court life: 'Very Trying: a record of a few trials of patience'.

1885 WG first appears on stage at the old Prince of Wales Theatre, Liverpool, as Specklebury in *Time Will Tell*. He joins Miss Rosina Vokes's company on a theatrical tour of the USA.

1887 WG returns to England; not an immediate success as an actor (his first London appearance is at the Gaiety as Woodcock in *Woodcock's Little Game*). He resumes painting.

1888 First instalment of *The Diary of a Nobody* published in *Punch*, 26 May 1888. GG publishes book of memoirs, *A Society Clown*. Henry Irving offers WG part of Jacques Strop in *Robert Macaire*: a success. WG's acting career in England takes off from this point.

1889 GG retires from the D'Oyly Carte company; returns to platform and piano performance, touring extensively in Britain and Ireland, the United States and Canada.

1891 WG plays in his own drama, *A Commission*, first at Terry's Theatre and then at the Shaftesbury Theatre.

1892 *The Diary of a Nobody* appears in book form.

1894 WG begins career as manager, at Terry's Theatre; then 1894–6 lessee and manager of the Vaudeville Theatre.

1895 WG marries May Palfrey: they have one daughter.

1896 WG publishes *A Woman with a History* (novel).

1901 WG's *The Night of the Party* staged. He becomes lessee of the Avenue Theatre: his acting career continues until at least 1914.

1903 WG's *The Cure* staged.

1905 Death of Emmeline Grossmith.

1907 GG converts to catholicism.

1908 GG retires from his performing career.

1910 GG publishes a further book of memoirs, *Piano and I*.

1912 1 March: GG dies.

1913 WG publishes *From Studio to Stage* (memoirs).

1919 14 June: WG dies.

The Diary of
a Nobody

Introduction by Mr Pooter

Why should I not publish my diary? I have often seen reminiscences of people I have never even heard of, and I fail to see—because I do not happen to be a 'Somebody'—why my diary should not be interesting. My only regret is that I did not commence it when I was a youth.

CHARLES POOTER

The Laurels,
Brickfield Terrace,
Holloway

CHAPTER I

We settle down in our new home, and I resolve to keep a diary. Tradesmen trouble us a bit, so does the scraper. The Curate calls and pays me a great compliment.

My dear wife Carrie and I have just been a week in our new house, 'The Laurels',* Brickfield Terrace, Holloway*—a nice six-roomed residence, not counting basement, with a front breakfast-parlour. We have a little front garden; and there is a flight of ten steps up to the front door, which, by-the-by, we keep locked with the chain up. Cummings, Gowing, and our other intimate friends always come to the little side entrance, which saves the servant the trouble of going up to the front door, thereby taking her from her work. We have a nice little back garden which runs down to the railway. We were rather afraid of the noise of the trains at first, but the landlord said we should not notice them after a bit, and took £2 off the rent. He was certainly right; and beyond the cracking of the garden wall at the bottom, we have suffered no inconvenience.

After my work in the City, I like to be at home. What's the good of a home, if you are never in it? 'Home, Sweet Home', that's my motto. I am always in of an evening. Our old friend Gowing may drop in without ceremony; so may Cummings, who lives opposite. My dear wife Caroline and I are pleased to see them, if they like to drop in on us. But Carrie and I can manage to pass our evenings together without friends. There is always something to be done: a tin-tack here, a Venetian blind to put straight, a fan to nail up, or part of a carpet to nail down—all of which I can do with my pipe in my mouth; while Carrie is not above putting a button on a shirt, mending a pillowcase, or practising the 'Sylvia Gavotte'* on our new cottage piano (on the three years' system), manufactured by W. Bilkson (in small letters), from Collard and Collard* (in very large letters). It is also a great comfort to us to know that our boy Willie is getting on so well in the Bank at Oldham. We should like to see more of him. Now for my diary:

APRIL 3.—Tradesmen called for custom, and I promised Farmerson, the ironmonger, to give him a turn if I wanted any nails or

The Laurels

tools. By-the-by, that reminds me there is no key to our bedroom door, and the bells must be seen to. The parlour bell is broken, and the front door rings up in the servant's bedroom, which is ridiculous. Dear friend Gowing dropped in, but wouldn't stay, saying there was an infernal smell of paint.

APRIL 4.—Tradesmen still calling; Carrie being out, I arranged to deal with Horwin, who seemed a civil butcher with a nice clean shop. Ordered a shoulder of mutton for tomorrow, to give him a trial. Carrie arranged with Borset, the butterman, and ordered a pound of fresh butter, and a pound and a half of salt ditto for kitchen, and a shilling's worth of eggs. In the evening, Cummings unexpectedly dropped in to show me a meerschaum* pipe he had won in a raffle in the City, and told me to handle it carefully, as it would spoil the colouring if the hand was moist. He said he wouldn't stay, as he didn't care much for the smell of the paint, and fell over the scraper as he went out. Must

Our dear friend Gowing

get the scraper removed, or else I shall get into a *scrape*. I don't often make jokes.

APRIL 5.—Two shoulders of mutton arrived, Carrie having arranged with another butcher without consulting me. Gowing called, and fell over scraper coming in. *Must* get that scraper removed.

APRIL 6.—Eggs for breakfast simply shocking; sent them back to Borset with my compliments, and he needn't call any more for orders. Couldn't find umbrella, and though it was pouring with rain, had to go without it. Sarah said Mr Gowing must have took it by mistake last night, as there was a stick in the 'all that didn't belong to nobody. In the evening, hearing someone talking in a loud voice to the servant in the downstairs hall, I went out to see who it was, and was surprised to find it was Borset, the butterman, who was both drunk and offensive. Borset, on seeing me, said he would be hanged if he would ever serve City clerks any more—the game wasn't worth the candle. I restrained

Our dear friend Cummings

my feelings, and quietly remarked that I thought it was *possible* for a
city clerk to be a *gentleman*. He replied he was very glad to hear it, and
wanted to know whether I had ever come across one, for *he* hadn't. He
left the house, slamming the door after him, which nearly broke the
fanlight; and I heard him fall over the scraper, which made me feel
glad I hadn't removed it. When he had gone, I thought of a splendid
answer I ought to have given him. However, I will keep it for another
occasion.

APRIL 7.—Being Saturday, I looked forward to being home early,
and putting a few things straight; but two of our principals at the

office were absent through illness, and I did not get home till seven. Found Borset waiting. He had been three times during the day to apologize for his conduct last night. He said he was unable to take his Bank Holiday last Monday, and took it last night instead. He begged me to accept his apology, and a pound of fresh butter. He seems, after all, a decent sort of fellow; so I gave him an order for some fresh eggs, with a request that on this occasion they *should* be fresh. I am afraid we shall have to get some new stair-carpets after all; our old ones are not quite wide enough to meet the paint on either side. Carrie suggests that we might ourselves broaden the paint. I will see if we can match the colour (dark chocolate) on Monday.

APRIL 8, SUNDAY.—After Church, the Curate came back with us. I sent Carrie in to open the front door, which we do not use except on special occasions. She could not get it open, and after all my display, I had to take the Curate (whose name, by-the-by, I did not catch) round the side entrance. He caught his foot in the scraper, and tore the bottom of his trousers. Most annoying, as Carrie could not well offer to repair them on a Sunday. After dinner, went to sleep. Took a walk round the garden, and discovered a beautiful spot for sowing mustard-and-cress and radishes. Went to Church again in the evening: walked back with the Curate. Carrie noticed he had got on the same pair of trousers, only repaired. He wants me to take round the plate, which I think a great compliment.

CHAPTER II

Tradesmen and the scraper still troublesome. Gowing rather tiresome with his complaints of the paint. I make one of the best jokes of my life. Delights of gardening. Mr Stillbrook, Gowing, Cummings, and I have a little mis-understanding. Sarah makes me look a fool before Cummings.

APRIL 9.—Commenced the morning badly. The butcher, whom we decided *not* to arrange with, called and blackguarded me in the most uncalled-for manner. He began by abusing me, and saying he did not want my custom. I simply said: 'Then what are you making all this fuss about it for?' And he shouted out at the top of his voice, so that all the neighbours could hear: 'Pah! go along. Ugh! I could buy up "things" like you by the dozen!'

I shut the door, and was giving Carrie to understand that this disgraceful scene was entirely her fault, when there was a violent kicking at the door, enough to break the panels. It was the blackguard butcher again, who said he had cut his foot over the scraper, and would immediately bring an action against me. Called at Farmerson's, the ironmonger, on my way to town, and gave him the job of moving the scraper and repairing the bells, thinking it scarcely worth while to trouble the landlord with such a trifling matter.

Arrived home tired and worried. Mr Putley, a painter and decorator, who had sent in a card, said he could not match the colour on the stairs, as it contained Indian carmine.* He said he spent half-a-day calling at warehouses to see if he could get it. He suggested he should entirely repaint the stairs. It would cost very little more; if he tried to match it, he could only make a bad job of it. It would be more satisfactory to him and to us to have the work done properly. I consented, but felt I had been talked over. Planted some mustard-and-cress and radishes, and went to bed at nine.

APRIL 10.—Farmerson came round to attend to the scraper himself. He seems a very civil fellow. He says he does not usually conduct such small jobs personally, but for *me* he would do so. I thanked him, and went to town. It is disgraceful how late some of the young clerks are at arriving. I told three of them that if Mr Perkupp, the principal, heard of it, they might be discharged.

Pitt, a monkey of seventeen, who has only been with us six weeks, told me 'to keep my hair on!' I informed him I had had the honour of being in the firm twenty years, to which he insolently replied that I 'looked it'. I gave him an indignant look, and said: 'I demand from you some respect, sir.' He replied: 'All right, go on demanding.' I would not argue with him any further. You cannot argue with people like that. In the evening Gowing called, and repeated his complaint about the smell of paint. Gowing is sometimes very tedious with his remarks, and not always cautious; and Carrie once very properly reminded him that she was present.

APRIL 11.—Mustard-and-cress and radishes not come up yet. To-day was a day of annoyances. I missed the quarter-to-nine 'bus to the City,* through having words with the grocer's boy, who for the second time had the impertinence to bring his basket to the hall-door, and had left the marks of his dirty boots on the fresh-cleaned doorsteps. He said he had knocked at the side door with his knuckles for a quarter of an hour. I knew Sarah, our servant, could not hear this, as she was upstairs doing the bedrooms, so asked the boy why he did not ring the bell? He replied that he did pull the bell, but the handle came off in his hand.

I was half-an-hour late at the office, a thing that has never happened to me before. There has recently been much irregularity in the attendance of the clerks, and Mr Perkupp, our principal, unfortunately chose this very morning to pounce down upon us early. Someone had given the tip to the others. The result was that I was the only one late of the lot. Buckling, one of the senior clerks, was a brick, and I was saved by his intervention. As I passed by Pitt's desk, I heard him remark to his neighbour: 'How disgracefully late some of the head clerks arrive!' This was, of course, meant for me. I treated the observation with silence, simply giving him a look, which unfortunately had the effect of making both of the clerks laugh. Thought afterwards it would have been more dignified if I had pretended not to have heard him at all. Cummings called in the evening, and we played dominoes.

APRIL 12.—Mustard-and-cress and radishes not come up yet. Left Farmerson repairing the scraper, but when I came home found three men working. I asked the meaning of it, and Farmerson said that in making a fresh hole he had penetrated the gas-pipe. He said it was a most ridiculous place to put the gas-pipe, and the man who did it evidently knew nothing about his business. I felt his excuse was no consolation for the expense I shall be put to.

In the evening, after tea, Gowing dropped in, and we had a smoke together in the breakfast-parlour. Carrie joined us later, but did not stay long, saying the smoke was too much for her. It was also rather too much for me, for Gowing had given me what he called a green cigar,* one that his friend Shoemach had just brought over from America. The cigar didn't look green, but I fancy I must have done so; for when I had smoked a little more than half I was obliged to retire on the pretext of telling Sarah to bring in the glasses.

I took a walk round the garden three or four times, feeling the need of fresh air. On returning Gowing noticed I was not smoking: offered me another cigar, which I politely declined. Gowing began his usual sniffing, so, anticipating him, I said: 'You're not going to complain of the smell of paint again?' He said: 'No, not this time; but I'll tell you what, I distinctly smell dry rot.' I don't often make jokes, but I replied: 'You're talking a lot of *dry rot* yourself.' I could not help roaring at this, and Carrie said her sides quite ached with laughter. I never was so immensely tickled by anything I had ever said before. I actually woke up twice during the night, and laughed till the bed shook.

APRIL 13.—An extraordinary coincidence: Carrie had called in a woman to make some chintz covers for our drawing-room chairs and sofa to prevent the sun fading the green rep* of the furniture. I saw the woman, and recognized her as a woman who used to work years ago for my old aunt at Clapham. It only shows how small the world is.

APRIL 14.—Spent the whole of the afternoon in the garden, having this morning picked up at a bookstall for fivepence a capital little book, in good condition, on *Gardening*. I procured and sowed some half-hardy annuals in what I fancy will be a warm, sunny border. I thought of a joke, and called out Carrie. Carrie came out rather testy, I thought. I said: 'I have just discovered we have got a lodging-house.' She replied: 'How do you mean?' I said: 'Look at the *boarders*.' Carrie said: 'Is that all you wanted me for?' I said: 'Any other time you would have laughed at my little pleasantry.' Carrie said: 'Certainly—*at any other time*, but not when I am busy in the house.' The stairs look very nice. Gowing called, and said the stairs looked *all right*, but it made the banisters look *all wrong*, and suggested a coat of paint on them also, which Carrie quite agreed with. I walked round to Putley, and fortunately he was out, so I had a good excuse to let the banisters slide. By-the-by, that is rather funny.

APRIL 15, SUNDAY.—At three o'clock Cummings and Gowing called for a good long walk over Hampstead and Finchley, and brought with them a friend named Stillbrook. We walked and chatted together, except Stillbrook, who was always a few yards behind us staring at the ground and cutting at the grass with his stick.

As it was getting on for five, we four held a consultation, and Gowing suggested that we should make for 'The Cow and Hedge' and get some tea. Stillbrook said: 'A brandy-and-soda was good enough for him.' I reminded them that all public-houses were closed till six o'clock. Stillbrook said, 'That's all right—bona fide travellers.'

We arrived; and as I was trying to pass, the man in charge of the gate said: 'Where from?' I replied: 'Holloway.' He immediately put up his arm, and declined to let me pass. I turned back for a moment, when I saw Stillbrook, closely followed by Cummings and Gowing, make for the entrance. I watched them, and thought I would have a good laugh at their expense. I heard the porter say: 'Where from?' When, to my surprise, in fact disgust, Stillbrook replied: 'Blackheath',* and the three were immediately admitted.

Gowing called to me across the gate, and said: 'We shan't be a minute.' I waited for them the best part of an hour. When they appeared they were all in most excellent spirits, and the only one who made an effort to apologize was Mr Stillbrook, who said to me: 'It was very rough on you to be kept waiting, but we had another spin for S. and B.'s.' I walked home in silence; I couldn't speak to them. I felt very dull all the evening, but deemed it advisable *not* to say anything to Carrie about the matter.

APRIL 16.—After business, set to work in the garden. When it got dark I wrote to Cummings and Gowing (who neither called, for a wonder; perhaps they were ashamed of themselves) about yesterday's adventure at 'The Cow and Hedge'. Afterwards made up my mind not to write *yet*.

Stillbrook lags behind. Going up hill

Going down hill

Nearly there

APRIL 17.—Thought I would write a kind little note to Gowing and Cummings about last Sunday, and warning them against Mr Stillbrook. Afterwards, thinking the matter over, tore up the letter and determined not to *write* at all, but to *speak* quietly to them. Dumbfounded at receiving a sharp letter from Cummings, saying that both he and Gowing had been waiting for an explanation of *my* (mind you, MY) extraordinary conduct coming home on Sunday. At last I wrote: 'I thought I was the aggrieved party; but as I freely forgive you, you—feeling yourself aggrieved—should bestow forgiveness on me.' I have copied this verbatim in the diary, because I think it is one of the most perfect and thoughtful sentences I have ever written. I

'Please, sir, the grocer says he ain't got no more Kinahan, but you'll find this very good at two-and-six.'

posted the letter, but in my own heart I felt I was actually apologizing for having been insulted.

APRIL 18.—Am in for a cold. Spent the whole day at the office sneezing. In the evening, the cold being intolerable, sent Sarah out for a bottle of Kinahan.* Fell asleep in the armchair, and woke with the shivers. Was startled by a loud knock at the front door. Carrie awfully flurried. Sarah still out, so went up, opened the door, and found it was only Cummings. Remembered the grocer's boy had again broken the side-bell. Cummings squeezed my hand, and said: 'I've just seen Gowing. All right. Say no more about it.' There is no doubt they are both under the impression I have apologized.

While playing dominoes with Cummings in the parlour, he said: 'By-the-by, do you want any wine or spirits? My cousin Merton has just set up in the trade, and has a splendid whisky, four years in bottle, at thirty-eight shillings. It is worth your while laying down a few dozen of it.' I told him my cellars, which were very small, were full up. To my horror, at that very moment, Sarah entered the room, and putting a bottle of whisky, wrapped in a dirty piece of newspaper, on the table in front of us, said: 'Please, sir, the grocer says he ain't got no more Kinahan, but you'll find this very good at two-and-six, with twopence returned on the bottle; and, please, did you want any more sherry? as he has some at one-and-three, as dry as a nut!'

CHAPTER III

A conversation with Mr Merton on Society. Mr and Mrs James, of Sutton, come up. A miserable evening at the Tank Theatre. Experiments with enamel paint. I make another good joke, but Gowing and Cummings are unnecessarily offended. I paint the bath red, with unexpected result.

APRIL 19.—Cummings called, bringing with him his friend Merton, who is in the wine trade. Gowing also called. Mr Merton made himself at home at once, and Carrie and I were both struck with him immediately; and thoroughly approved of his sentiments.

He leaned back in his chair and said: 'You must take me as I am'; and I replied: 'Yes—and you must take us as we are. We're homely people, we are not swells.'

He answered: 'No, I can see that,' and Gowing roared with laughter; but Merton in a most gentlemanly manner said to Gowing: 'I don't think you quite understand me. I intended to convey that our charming host and hostess were superior to the follies of fashion, and preferred leading a simple and wholesome life to gadding about to twopenny-halfpenny tea-drinking afternoons, and living above their incomes.'

I was immensely pleased with these sensible remarks of Merton's, and concluded that subject by saying: 'No, candidly, Mr Merton, we don't go into Society, because we do not care for it; and what with the expense of cabs here and cabs there, and white gloves and white ties, etc., it doesn't seem worth the money.'

Merton said in reference to *friends*: 'My motto is "Few and True"; and, by the way, I also apply that to wine, "Little and Good"'. Gowing said: 'Yes, and sometimes "cheap and tasty", eh, old man?' Merton, still continuing, said he should treat me as a friend, and put me down for a dozen of his 'Lockanbar' whisky, and as I was an old friend of Gowing, I should have it for 36s., which was considerably under what he paid for it.

He booked his own order, and further said that at any time I wanted any passes for the theatre I was to let him know, as his name stood good for any theatre in London.

APRIL 20.—Carrie reminded me that as her old school friend, Annie Fullers (now Mrs James), and her husband had come up from Sutton* for a few days, it would look kind to take them to the theatre, and would I drop a line to Mr Merton asking him for passes for four, either for the Italian Opera, Haymarket, Savoy, or Lyceum.* I wrote Merton to that effect.

APRIL 21.—Got a reply from Merton, saying he was very busy, and just at present couldn't manage passes for the Italian Opera, Haymarket, Savoy, or Lyceum, but the best thing going on in London was the *Brown Bushes*, at the Tank Theatre, Islington,* and enclosed seats for four; also bill for whisky.

APRIL 23.—Mr and Mrs James (Miss Fullers that was) came to meat-tea, and we left directly after for the Tank Theatre. We got a 'bus that took us to King's Cross, and then changed into one that took us to the 'Angel'.* Mr James each time insisted on paying for all, saying that I had paid for the tickets and that was quite enough.

We arrived at theatre, where, curiously enough, all our 'bus-load except an old woman with a basket seemed to be going in. I walked ahead and presented the tickets. The man looked at them, and called out: 'Mr Willowly! do you know anything about these?' holding up my tickets. The gentleman called to came up and examined my tickets, and said: 'Who gave you these?' I said, rather indignantly: 'Mr Merton, of course.' He said: 'Merton? Who's he?' I answered, rather sharply: 'You ought to know, his name's good at any theatre in London.' He replied: 'Oh! is it? Well, it ain't no good here. These tickets, which are *not* dated, were issued under Mr Swinstead's management, which has since changed hands.' While I was having some very unpleasant words with the man, James, who had gone upstairs with the ladies, called out: 'Come on!' I went up after them, and a very civil attendant said: 'This way, please, box H.' I said to James: 'Why, how on earth did you manage it?' and to my horror he replied: 'Why, paid for it of course.'

This was humiliating enough, and I could scarcely follow the play, but I was doomed to still further humiliation. I was leaning out of the box, when my tie—a little black bow which fastened on to the stud by means of a new patent—fell into the pit below. A clumsy man not noticing it, had his foot on it for ever so long before he discovered it.

He then picked it up and eventually flung it under the next seat in disgust. What with the box incident and the tie, I felt quite miserable. Mr James, of Sutton, was very good. He said: 'Don't worry—no one will notice it with your beard. That is the only advantage of growing one that I can see.' There was no occasion for that remark, for Carrie is very proud of my beard.

To hide the absence of the tie I had to keep my chin down the rest of the evening, which caused a pain at the back of my neck.

APRIL 24.—Could scarcely sleep a wink through thinking of having brought up Mr and Mrs James from the country to go to the theatre last night, and his having paid for a private box because our order was not honoured; and such a poor play too. I wrote a very satirical letter to Merton, the wine merchant, who gave us the pass, and said, 'Considering we had to *pay* for our seats, we did our *best* to appreciate the performance.' I thought this line rather cutting, and I asked Carrie how many p's there were in appreciate, and she said, 'One'. After I sent off the letter I looked at the dictionary and found there were two. Awfully vexed at this.

Decided not to worry myself any more about the James's; for, as Carrie wisely said, 'We'll make it all right with them by asking them up from Sutton one evening next week to play at Bézique.'*

APRIL 25.—In consequence of Brickwell telling me his wife was working wonders with the new Pinkford's enamel paint, I determined to try it. I bought two tins of red on my way home. I hastened through tea, went into the garden and painted some flowerpots. I called out Carrie, who said: 'You've always got some new-fangled craze'; but she was obliged to admit that the flowerpots looked remarkably well. Went upstairs into the servant's bedroom and painted her washstand, towel-horse, and chest of drawers. To my mind it was an extraordinary improvement, but as an example of the ignorance of the lower classes in the matter of taste, our servant, Sarah, on seeing them, evinced no sign of pleasure, but merely said 'she thought they looked very well as they was before'.

APRIL 26.—Got some more red enamel paint (red, to my mind, being the best colour), and painted the coal-scuttle, and the backs of our *Shakespeare*, the binding of which had almost worn out.

APRIL 27.—Painted the bath red, and was delighted with the result. Sorry to say Carrie was not, in fact we had a few words about it. She said I ought to have consulted her, and she had never heard of such a thing as a bath being painted red. I replied: 'It's merely a matter of taste.'

Fortunately, further argument on the subject was stopped by a voice saying, 'May I come in?' It was only Cummings, who said, 'Your maid opened the door, and asked me to excuse her showing me in, as she was wringing out some socks.' I was delighted to see him, and suggested we should have a game of whist with a dummy, and by way of merriment said: '*You* can be the dummy.' Cummings (I thought rather ill-naturedly) replied: 'Funny as usual.' He said he couldn't stop, he only called to leave me the *Bicycle News*,* as he had done with it.

I painted the washstand in the servant's bedroom.

Another ring at the bell; it was Gowing, who said he 'must apologize for coming so often, and that one of these days *we* must come round to *him*'. I said: 'A very extraordinary thing has struck me.' 'Something funny, as usual,' said Cummings. 'Yes,' I replied; 'I think even *you* will say so this time. It's concerning you both; for doesn't it seem odd that Gowing's always *coming* and Cummings always *going*?' Carrie, who had evidently quite forgotten about the bath, went into fits of laughter, and as for myself, I fairly doubled up in my chair, till it cracked beneath me. I think this was one of the best jokes I have ever made.

Then imagine my astonishment on perceiving both Cummings and Gowing perfectly silent, and without a smile on their faces. After rather an unpleasant pause, Cummings, who had opened a cigar-case, closed it up again and said: 'Yes—I think, after that, I *shall* be going, and I am sorry I fail to see the fun of your jokes.' Gowing said he didn't mind a joke when it wasn't rude, but a pun on a name, to his thinking, was certainly a little wanting in good taste. Cummings followed it up by saying, if it had been said by anyone else but myself, he shouldn't have entered the house again. This rather unpleasantly terminated what might have been a cheerful evening. However, it was as well they went, for the charwoman had finished up the remains of the cold pork.

APRIL 28.—At the office, the new and very young clerk Pitt, who was very impudent to me a week or so ago, was late again. I told him it would be my duty to inform Mr Perkupp, the principal. To my surprise, Pitt apologized most humbly and in a most gentlemanly fashion. I was unfeignedly pleased to notice this improvement in his manner towards me, and told him I would look over his unpunctuality. Passing down the room an hour later I received a smart smack in the face from a rolled-up ball of hard foolscap. I turned round sharply, but all the clerks were apparently riveted to their work. I am not a rich man, but I would give half-a-sovereign* to know whether that was thrown by accident or design. Went home early and bought some more enamel paint—black this time—and spent the evening touching up the fender, picture-frames, and an old pair of boots, making them look as good as new. Also painted Gowing's walking-stick, which he left behind, and made it look like ebony.

'I looked like Marat in the bath, in Madame Tussaud's.'

APRIL 29, SUNDAY.—Woke up with a fearful headache and strong symptoms of a cold. Carrie, with a perversity which is just like her, said it was 'painter's colic', and was the result of my having spent the last few days with my nose over a paint-pot. I told her firmly that I knew a great deal better what was the matter with me than she did. I had got a chill, and decided to have a bath as hot as I could bear it. Bath ready—could scarcely bear it so hot. I persevered, and got in; very hot, but very acceptable. I lay still for some time.

On moving my hand above the surface of the water, I experienced the greatest fright I ever received in the whole course of my life; for imagine my horror on discovering my hand, as I thought, full of blood. My first thought was that I had ruptured an artery, and was bleeding to death, and should be discovered, later on, looking like a second Marat,* as I remember seeing him in Madame Tussaud's.* My second thought was to ring the bell, but remembered there was no bell to ring. My third was, that there was nothing but the enamel paint, which had dissolved with boiling water. I stepped out of the bath, perfectly red all over, resembling the Red Indians I have seen depicted at an East-End theatre. I determined not to say a word to Carrie, but to tell Farmerson to come on Monday and paint the bath white.

CHAPTER IV

The ball at the Mansion House

APRIL 30.—Perfectly astounded at receiving an invitation for Carrie and myself from the Lord and Lady Mayoress to the Mansion House,* to 'meet the Representatives of Trades and Commerce'. My heart beat like that of a schoolboy's. Carrie and I read the invitation over two or three times. I could scarcely eat my breakfast. I said—and I felt it from the bottom of my heart—'Carrie darling, I was a proud man when I led you down the aisle of the church on our wedding day; that pride will be equalled, if not surpassed, when I lead my dear, pretty wife up to the Lord and Lady Mayoress at the Mansion House.' I saw the tears in Carrie's eyes, and she said: 'Charlie dear, it is *I* who have to be proud of you. And I am very, very proud of you. You have called me pretty; and as long as I am pretty in your eyes, I am happy. You, dear old Charlie, are *not* handsome, but you are *good*, which is far more noble.' I gave her a kiss, and she said: 'I wonder if there will be any dancing? I have not danced with you for years.'

I cannot tell what induced me to do it, but I seized her round the waist, and we were silly enough to be executing a wild kind of polka when Sarah entered, grinning, and said: 'There is a man, mum, at the door who wants to know if you want any good coals.' Most annoyed at this. Spent the evening in answering, and tearing up again, the reply to the Mansion House, having left word with Sarah if Gowing or Cummings called we were not at home. Must consult Mr Perkupp how to answer the Lord Mayor's invitation.

MAY 1.—Carrie said: 'I should like to send mother the invitation to look at.' I consented, as soon as I had answered it. I told Mr Perkupp, at the office, with a feeling of pride, that we had received an invitation to the Mansion House; and he said, to my astonishment, that he himself gave in my name to the Lord Mayor's secretary. I felt this rather discounted the value of the invitation, but I thanked him; and in reply to me, he described how I was to answer it. I felt the reply was too simple; but of course Mr Perkupp knows best.

'I seized her round the waist, and we were silly enough to be executing a wild kind of polka when Sarah entered.'

MAY 2.—Sent my dress-coat and trousers to the little tailor's round the corner, to have the creases taken out. Told Gowing not to call next Monday, as we were going to the Mansion House. Sent similar note to Cummings.

MAY 3.—Carrie went to Mrs James, at Sutton, to consult about her dress for next Monday. While speaking incidentally to Spotch, one of our head clerks, about the Mansion House, he said: 'Oh, I'm asked, but don't think I shall go.' When a vulgar man like Spotch is asked I feel my invitation is considerably discounted. In the evening, while I was out, the little tailor brought round my coat and trousers, and because Sarah had not a shilling to pay for the pressing, he took them away again.

MAY 4.—Carrie's mother returned the Lord Mayor's invitation, which was sent to her to look at, with apologies for having upset a glass of port over it. I was too angry to say anything.

MAY 5.—Bought a pair of lavender kid-gloves for next Monday, and two white ties, in case one got spoiled in the tying.

MAY 6, SUNDAY.—A very dull sermon, during which, I regret to say, I twice thought of the Mansion House reception tomorrow.

MAY 7.—A big red-letter day; viz., the Lord Mayor's reception. The whole house upset. I had to get dressed at half-past six, as Carrie wanted the room to herself. Mrs James had come up from Sutton to help Carrie; so I could not help thinking it unreasonable that she should require the entire attention of Sarah, the servant, as well. Sarah kept running out of the house to fetch 'something for missis', and several times I had, in my full evening-dress, to answer the back-door.

The last time it was the greengrocer's boy, who, not seeing it was me, for Sarah had not lighted the gas, pushed into my hands two cabbages and half-a-dozen coal-blocks. I indignantly threw them on the ground, and felt so annoyed that I so far forgot myself as to box the boy's ears. He went away crying, and said he should summons me, a thing I would not have happen for the world. In the dark, I stepped on a piece of the cabbage, which brought me down on the flags all of a heap. For a moment I was stunned, but when I recovered I crawled upstairs into the drawing-room and on looking into the chimney-glass* discovered that my chin was bleeding, my shirt smeared with the coal-blocks, and my left trouser torn at the knee.

However, Mrs James brought me down another shirt, which I changed in the drawing-room. I put a piece of court-plaster on my chin, and Sarah very neatly sewed up the tear at the knee. At nine o'clock Carrie swept into the room, looking like a queen. Never have I seen her look so lovely, or so distinguished. She was wearing a satin dress of sky-blue—my favourite colour—and a piece of lace, which Mrs James lent her, round the shoulders, to give a finish. I thought perhaps the dress was a little too long behind, and decidedly too short in front, but Mrs James said it was à la mode. Mrs James was most kind, and lent Carrie a fan of ivory with red feathers, the value of

'*The greengrocer's boy . . . who pushed into my hands two cabbages and half-a-dozen coal-blocks.*'

which, she said, was priceless, as the feathers belonged to the Kachu eagle*—a bird now extinct. I preferred the little white fan which Carrie bought for three-and-six at Shoolbred's,* but both ladies sat on me at once.

We arrived at the Mansion House too early, which was rather fortunate, for I had an opportunity of speaking to his lordship, who graciously condescended to talk with me some minutes; but I must say I was disappointed to find he did not even know Mr Perkupp, the principal.

I felt as if we had been invited to the Mansion House by one who did not know the Lord Mayor himself. Crowds arrived, and I shall never forget the grand sight. My humble pen can never describe it. I was a little annoyed with Carrie, who kept saying: 'Isn't it a pity we don't know anybody?'

Once she quite lost her head. I saw someone who looked like Franching, from Peckham, and was moving towards him when she seized me by the coat-tails, and said quite loudly: 'Don't leave me,' which caused an elderly gentleman, in a court-suit, and a chain round him, and two ladies, to burst out laughing. There was an immense crowd in the supper-room, and, my stars! it was a splendid supper— any amount of champagne.

Carrie made a most hearty supper, for which I was pleased; for I sometimes think she is not strong. There was scarcely a dish she did not taste. I was so thirsty, I could not eat much. Receiving a sharp slap on the shoulder, I turned, and, to my amazement, saw Farmerson, our ironmonger. He said, in the most familiar way: 'This is better than Brickfield Terrace, eh?' I simply looked at him, and said coolly: 'I never expected to see you here.' He said, with a loud, coarse laugh: 'I like that—if *you*, why not *me*?' I replied: 'Certainly.' I wish I could have thought of something better to say. He said: 'Can I get your good lady anything?' Carrie said: 'No, I thank you,' for which I was pleased. I said, by way of reproof to him: 'You never sent today to paint the bath, as I requested.' Farmerson said: 'Pardon me, Mr Pooter, no shop when we're in company, please.'

Before I could think of a reply, one of the sheriffs, in full Court costume, slapped Farmerson on the back and hailed him as an old friend, and asked him to dine with him at his lodge.* I was astonished. For full five minutes they stood roaring with laughter, and stood digging each other in the ribs. They kept telling each other they didn't look a day older. They began embracing each other and drink- ing champagne.

To think that a man who mends our scraper should know any member of our aristocracy! I was just moving with Carrie, when Farmerson seized me rather roughly by the collar, and addressing the sheriff, said: 'Let me introduce my neighbour, Pooter.' He did not even say 'Mister'. The sheriff handed me a glass of champagne. I felt, after all, it was a great honour to drink a glass of wine with him, and I told him so. We stood chatting for some time, and at last I said: 'You must excuse me now if I join Mrs Pooter.' When I approached her, she said: 'Don't let me take you away from friends. I am quite happy standing here alone in a crowd, knowing nobody!'

As it takes two to make a quarrel, and as it was neither the time nor the place for it, I gave my arm to Carrie, and said: 'I hope my darling little wife will dance with me, if only for the sake of saying we had danced at the Mansion House as guests of the Lord Mayor.' Finding the dancing after supper was less formal, and knowing how much Carrie used to admire my dancing in the days gone by, I put my arm round her waist and we commenced a waltz.

A most unfortunate accident occurred. I had got on a new pair of boots. Foolishly, I had omitted to take Carrie's advice; namely, to scratch the soles of them with the points of the scissors or to put a little wet on them. I had scarcely started when, like lightning, my left foot slipped away and I came down, the side of my head striking the floor with such violence that for a second or two I did not know what had happened. I need hardly say that Carrie fell with me with equal violence, breaking the comb in her hair and grazing her elbow.

There was a roar of laughter, which was immediately checked when people found that we had really hurt ourselves. A gentleman assisted Carrie to a seat, and I expressed myself pretty strongly on the danger of having a plain polished floor with no carpet or drugget to prevent people slipping. The gentleman, who said his name was Darwitts, insisted on escorting Carrie to have a glass of wine, an invitation which I was pleased to allow Carrie to accept.

I followed, and met Farmerson, who immediately said, in his loud voice: 'Oh, are you the one who went down?'

I answered with an indignant look.

With execrable taste, he said: 'Look here, old man, we are too old for this game. We must leave these capers to the youngsters. Come and have another glass, that is more in our line.'

Although I felt I was buying his silence by accepting, we followed the others into the supper-room.

Neither Carrie nor I, after our unfortunate mishap, felt inclined to stay longer. As we were departing, Farmerson said: 'Are you going? if so, you might give me a lift.'

I thought it better to consent, but wish I had first consulted Carrie.

CHAPTER V

After the Mansion House Ball. Carrie offended. Gowing also offended. A pleasant party at the Cummings's. Mr Franching, of Peckham, visits us.

MAY 8.—I woke up with a most terrible headache. I could scarcely see, and the back of my neck was as if I had given it a crick. I thought first of sending for a doctor; but I did not think it necessary. When up, I felt faint, and went to Brownish's, the chemist, who gave me a draught. So bad at the office, had to get leave to come home. Went to another chemist in the City, and I got a draught. Brownish's dose seems to have made me worse; have eaten nothing all day. To make matters worse, Carrie, every time I spoke to her, answered me sharply—that is, when she answered at all.

In the evening I felt very much worse again and said to her: 'I do believe I've been poisoned by the lobster mayonnaise at the Mansion House last night'; she simply replied, without taking her eyes from her sewing: 'Champagne never did agree with you.' I felt irritated, and said: 'What nonsense you talk; I only had a glass and a half, and you know as well as I do——' Before I could complete the sentence she bounced out of the room. I sat over an hour waiting for her to return; but as she did not, I determined I would go to bed. I discovered Carrie had gone to bed without even saying 'good-night'; leaving me to bar the scullery door and feed the cat. I shall certainly speak to her about this in the morning.

MAY 9.—Still a little shaky, with black specks. The *Blackfriars Bi-weekly News* contains a long list of the guests at the Mansion House Ball. Disappointed to find our names omitted, though Farmerson's is in plainly enough with M.L.L.* after it, whatever that may mean. More than vexed, because we had ordered a dozen copies to send to our friends. Wrote to the *Blackfriars Bi-weekly News*, pointing out their omission.

Carrie had commenced her breakfast when I entered the parlour. I helped myself to a cup of tea, and I said, perfectly calmly and quietly: 'Carrie, I wish a little explanation of your conduct last night.'

She replied, 'Indeed! and I desire something more than a *little* explanation of your conduct the night before.'

I said, coolly: 'Really, I don't understand you.'

Carrie said sneeringly: 'Probably not; you were scarcely in a condition to understand anything.'

I was astounded at this insinuation and simply ejaculated: 'Caroline!'

She said: 'Don't be theatrical, it has no effect on me. Reserve that tone for your new friend, *Mister* Farmerson, the ironmonger.'

I was about to speak, when Carrie, in a temper such as I have never seen her in before, told me to hold my tongue. She said: 'Now *I'm* going to say something! After professing to snub Mr Farmerson, you permit him to snub *you*, in my presence, and then accept his invitation to take a glass of champagne with you, and you don't limit yourself to one glass. You then offer this vulgar man, who made a

Mr Farmerson smokes all the way home in the cab

bungle of repairing our scraper, a seat in our cab on the way home. I say nothing about his tearing my dress in getting in the cab, nor of treading on Mrs James's expensive fan, which you knocked out of my hand, and for which he never even apologized; but you smoked all the way home without having the decency to ask my permission. That is not all! At the end of the journey, although he did not offer you a farthing towards his share of the cab, you asked him in. Fortunately, he was sober enough to detect, from my manner, that his company was not desirable.'

Goodness knows I felt humiliated enough at this; but, to make matters worse, Gowing entered the room, without knocking, with two hats on his head and holding the garden-rake in his hand, with Carrie's fur tippet (which he had taken off the downstairs hall-peg) round his neck, and announced himself in a loud, coarse voice: 'His Royal Highness, the Lord Mayor!' He marched twice round the room like a buffoon, and finding we took no notice, said: 'Hulloh! what's up? Lovers' quarrel, eh?'

There was a silence for a moment, so I said quietly: 'My dear Gowing, I'm not very well, and not quite in the humour for joking; especially when you enter the room without knocking, an act which I fail to see the fun of.'

Gowing said: 'I'm very sorry, but I called for my stick, which I thought you would have sent round.' I handed him his stick, which I remembered I had painted black with the enamel paint, thinking to improve it. He looked at it for a minute with a dazed expression and said: 'Who did this?'

I said: 'Eh, did what?'

He said: 'Did what? Why, destroyed my stick! It belonged to my poor uncle, and I value it more than anything I have in the world! I'll know who did it.'

I said: 'I'm very sorry. I dare say it will come off. I did it for the best.'

Gowing said: 'Then all I can say is, it's a confounded liberty; and I *would* add, you're a bigger fool than you look, only *that's* absolutely impossible.'

MAY 12.—Got a single copy of the *Blackfriars Bi-weekly News*. There was a short list of several names they had omitted; but the stupid people had mentioned our names as 'Mr and Mrs C. Porter'. Most annoying! Wrote again and I took particular care to write our name in capital letters, *POOTER*, so that there should be no possible mistake this time.

MAY 16.—Absolutely disgusted on opening the *Blackfriars Bi-weekly News* of today, to find the following paragraph: 'We have received two letters from Mr and Mrs Charles Pewter, requesting us to announce the important fact that they were at the Mansion House Ball.' I tore up the paper and threw it in the waste-paper basket. My time is far too valuable to bother about such trifles.

MAY 21.—The last week or ten days terribly dull, Carrie being away at Mrs James's, at Sutton. Cummings also away. Gowing, I presume, is still offended with me for black-enamelling his stick without asking him.

MAY 22.—Purchased a new stick mounted with silver, which cost seven-and-sixpence (shall tell Carrie five shillings), and sent it round with nice note to Gowing.

MAY 23.—Received strange note from Gowing; he said: 'Offended? not a bit, my boy. I thought you were offended with me for losing my temper. Besides, I found after all, it was not my poor old uncle's stick you painted. It was only a shilling thing I bought at a tobacconist's. However, I am much obliged to you for your handsome present all the same.'

MAY 24.—Carrie back. Hoorah! She looks wonderfully well, except that the sun has caught her nose.

MAY 25.—Carrie brought down some of my shirts and advised me to take them to Trillip's round the corner. She said: 'The fronts and cuffs are much frayed.' I said without a moment's hesitation: 'I'm *frayed* they are.' Lor! how we roared. I thought we should never stop laughing. As I happened to be sitting next the driver going to town on the 'bus, I told him my joke about the 'frayed' shirts. I thought he would have rolled off his seat. They laughed at the office a good bit too over it.

MAY 26.—Left the shirts to be repaired at Trillip's. I said to him: 'I'm *'fraid* they are *frayed*.' He said, without a smile: 'They're bound to do that, sir.' Some people seem to be quite destitute of a sense of humour.

JUNE 1.—The last week has been like old times, Carrie being back, and Gowing and Cummings calling every evening nearly. Twice we sat out in the garden quite late. This evening we were like a pack of children, and played 'consequences'.* It is a good game.

JUNE 2.—'Consequences' again this evening. Not quite so successful as last night; Gowing having several times overstepped the limits of good taste.

JUNE 4.—In the evening Carrie and I went round to Mr and Mrs Cummings's to spend a quiet evening with them. Gowing was there, also Mr Stillbrook. It was quiet but pleasant. Mrs Cummings sang five or six songs, 'No, Sir', and 'The Garden of Sleep',* being best in my humble judgement; but what pleased me most was the duet she sang with Carrie—classical duet, too. I think it is called, 'I would that my love!' It was beautiful. If Carrie had been in better voice, I don't think professionals could have sung it better. After supper we made them sing it again. I never liked Mr Stillbrook since the walk that Sunday to the 'Cow and Hedge', but I must say he sings comic-songs well. His song: 'We don't want the old men now', made us shriek with laughter, especially the verse referring to Mr Gladstone;* but there was one verse I think he might have omitted, and I said so, but Gowing thought it was the best of the lot.

JUNE 6.—Trillip brought round the shirts and, to my disgust, his charge for repairing was more than I gave for them when new. I told him so, and he impertinently replied: 'Well, they are better now than when they were new.' I paid him, and said it was a robbery. He said: 'If you wanted your shirt-fronts made out of pauper-linen, such as is used for packing and book-binding, why didn't you say so?'

JUNE 7.—A dreadful annoyance. Met Mr Franching, who lives at Peckham, and who is a great swell in his way. I ventured to ask him to come home to meat-tea, and take pot-luck. I did not think he would accept such a humble invitation; but he did, saying, in a most friendly way, he would rather 'peck' with us than by himself. I said: 'We had better get into this blue 'bus.' He replied: 'No blue-bussing

Mr Franching, of Peckham

for me. I have had enough of the blues lately. I lost a cool "thou" over the Copper Scare. Step in here.'

We drove up home in style, in a hansom-cab, and I knocked three times at the front door without getting an answer. I saw Carrie, through the panels of ground-glass (with stars), rushing upstairs. I told Mr Franching to wait at the door while I went round to the side. There I saw the grocer's boy actually picking off the paint on the door, which had formed into blisters. No time to reprove him; so went round and effected an entrance through the kitchen window. I let in Mr Franching, and showed him into the drawing-room. I went up-

stairs to Carrie, who was changing her dress, and told her I had
persuaded Mr Franching to come home. She replied: 'How can you
do such a thing? You know it's Sarah's holiday, and there's not a thing
in the house, the cold mutton having turned with the hot weather.'

Eventually Carrie, like a good creature as she is, slipped down,
washed up the teacups, and laid the cloth, and I gave Franching our
views of Japan* to look at while I ran round to the butcher's to get
three chops.

JULY 30.—The miserable cold weather is either upsetting me or
Carrie, or both. We seem to break out into an argument about abso-

*The grocer boy was actually picking off the paint on the side door, which had
formed into blisters*

lutely nothing, and this unpleasant state of things usually occurs at meal-times.

This morning, for some unaccountable reason, we were talking about balloons, and we were as merry as possible; but the conversation drifted into family matters, during which Carrie, without the slightest reason, referred in the most uncomplimentary manner to my poor father's pecuniary trouble. I retorted by saying that 'Pa, at all events, was a gentleman,' whereupon Carrie burst out crying. I positively could not eat any breakfast.

At the office I was sent for by Mr Perkupp, who said he was very sorry, but I should have to take my annual holidays from next Saturday. Franching called at office and asked me to dine at his club, 'The Constitutional'. Fearing disagreeables at home after the 'tiff' this morning, I sent a telegram to Carrie, telling her I was going out to dine and she was not to sit up. Bought a little silver bangle for Carrie.

JULY 31.—Carrie was very pleased with the bangle, which I left with an affectionate note on her dressing-table last night before going to bed. I told Carrie we should have to start for our holiday next Saturday. She replied quite happily that she did not mind, except that the weather was so bad, and she feared that Miss Jibbons would not be able to get her a seaside dress in time. I told Carrie that I thought the drab one with pink bows looked quite good enough; and Carrie said she should not think of wearing it. I was about to discuss the matter, when, remembering the argument yesterday, resolved to hold my tongue.

I said to Carrie: 'I don't think we can do better than "Good old Broadstairs".' Carrie not only, to my astonishment, raised an objection to Broadstairs, for the first time; but begged me not to use the expression, 'Good old', but to leave it to Mr Stillbrook and other *gentlemen* of his type. Hearing my 'bus pass the window, I was obliged to rush out of the house without kissing Carrie as usual; and I shouted to her: 'I leave it to you to decide.' On returning in the evening, Carrie said she thought as the time was so short she had decided on Broadstairs, and had written to Mrs Beck, Harbour View Terrace, for apartments.

AUGUST 1.—Ordered a new pair of trousers at Edwards's, and told them not to cut them so loose over the boot; the last pair being so

Young Pitt called out 'Hornpipe', as I passed his desk

loose and also tight at the knee, looked like a sailor's, and I heard Pitt,
that objectionable youth at the office, call out 'Hornpipe' as I passed
his desk. Carrie was ordered of Miss Jibbons a pink Garibaldi* and
blue-serge skirt, which I always think looks so pretty at the seaside.
In the evening she trimmed herself a little sailor-hat, while I read to
her the *Exchange and Mart.** We had a good laugh over my trying on
the hat when she had finished it; Carrie saying it looked so funny with
my beard, and how the people would have roared if I went on the
stage like it.

AUGUST 2.—Mrs Beck wrote to say we could have our usual rooms
at Broadstairs. That's off our mind. Bought a coloured shirt and a pair
of tan-coloured boots, which I see many of the swell clerks wearing in
the City, and hear are all the 'go'.

AUGUST 3.—A beautiful day. Looking forward to tomorrow. Carrie
bought a parasol about five feet long. I told her it was ridiculous. She

said: 'Mrs James, of Sutton, has one twice as long'; so the matter dropped. I bought a capital hat for hot weather at the seaside. I don't know what it is called, but it is the shape of the helmet worn in India,* only made of straw. Got three new ties, two coloured handkerchiefs, and a pair of navy-blue socks at Pope Brothers. Spent the evening packing. Carrie told me not to forget to borrow Mr Higgsworth's telescope, which he always lends me, knowing I know how to take care of it. Sent Sarah out for it. While everything was seeming so bright, the last post brought us a letter from Mrs Beck, saying: 'I have just let all my house to one party, and am sorry I must take back my words, and am sorry you must find other apartments; but Mrs Womming, next door, will be pleased to accommodate you, but she cannot take you before Monday, as her rooms are engaged Bank Holiday week.'

CHAPTER VI

The Unexpected Arrival Home of our Son, Willie Lupin Pooter

AUGUST 4.—The first post brought a nice letter from our dear son Willie, acknowledging a trifling present which Carrie sent him, the day before yesterday being his twentieth birthday. To our utter amazement he turned up himself in the afternoon, having journeyed all the way from Oldham. He said he had got leave from the bank, and as Monday was a holiday he thought he would give us a little surprise.

AUGUST 5, SUNDAY.—We have not seen Willie since last Christmas, and are pleased to notice what a fine young man he has grown. One would scarcely believe he was Carrie's son. He looks more like a younger brother. I rather disapprove of his wearing a check suit on a Sunday, and I think he ought to have gone to church this morning; but he said he was tired after yesterday's journey, so I refrained from any remark on the subject. We had a bottle of port for dinner, and drank dear Willie's health.

He said: 'Oh, by-the-by, did I tell you I've cut my first name, "William", and taken the second name "Lupin"? In fact, I'm only known at Oldham as "Lupin Pooter". If you were to "Willie" me there, they wouldn't know what you meant.'

Of course, Lupin being a purely family name, Carrie was delighted, and began by giving a long history of the Lupins. I ventured to say that I thought William a nice simple name, and reminded him he was christened after his Uncle William, who was much respected in the City. Willie, in a manner which I did not much care for, said sneeringly: 'Oh, I know all about that—Good old Bill!' and helped himself to a third glass of port.

Carrie objected strongly to my saying 'Good old', but she made no remark when Willie used the double adjective. I said nothing, but looked at her, which meant more. I said: 'My dear Willie, I hope you are happy with your colleagues at the Bank.' He replied: 'Lupin, if you please; and with respect to the Bank, there's not a clerk who is a gentleman, and the "boss" is a cad.' I felt so shocked, I could say nothing, and my instinct told me there was something wrong.

AUGUST 6, BANK HOLIDAY.—As there was no sign of Lupin moving at nine o'clock, I knocked at his door, and said we usually breakfasted at half-past eight, and asked how long would he be? Lupin replied that he had had a lively time of it, first with the train shaking the house all night, and then with the sun streaming in through the window in his eyes, and giving him a cracking headache. Carrie came up and asked if he would like some breakfast sent up, and he said he could do with a cup of tea, and didn't want anything to eat.

Lupin not having come down, I went up again at half-past one, and said we dined at two; he said he 'would be there'. He never came down till a quarter to three. I said: 'We have not seen much of you, and you will have to return by the 5.30 train; therefore you will have to leave in an hour, unless you go by the midnight mail.' He said:

Lupin

'Look here, Guv'nor, it's no use beating about the bush. I've tendered my resignation at the Bank.'

For a moment I could not speak. When my speech came again, I said: 'How dare you, sir? How dare you take such a serious step without consulting me? Don't answer me, sir!—you will sit down immediately, and write a note at my dictation, withdrawing your resignation and amply apologizing for your thoughtlessness.'

Imagine my dismay when he replied with a loud guffaw: 'It's no use. If you want the good old truth, I've got the chuck!'*

AUGUST 7.—Mr Perkupp has given me leave to postpone my holiday a week, as we could not get the room. This will give us an opportunity of trying to find an appointment for Willie before we go. The ambition of my life would be to get him into Mr Perkupp's firm.

AUGUST 11.—Although it is a serious matter having our boy Lupin on our hands, still it is satisfactory to know he was asked to resign from the Bank simply because 'he took no interest in his work, and always arrived an hour (sometimes two hours) late'. We can all start off on Monday to Broadstairs with a light heart. This will take my mind off the worry of the last few days, which have been wasted over a useless correspondence with the manager of the Bank at Oldham.

AUGUST 13.—Hurrah! at Broadstairs. Very nice apartments near the station. On the cliffs they would have been double the price. The landlady had a nice five o'clock dinner and tea ready, which we all enjoyed, though Lupin seemed fastidious because there happened to be a fly in the butter. It was very wet in the evening, for which I was thankful, as it was a good excuse for going to bed early. Lupin said he would sit up and read a bit.

AUGUST 14.—I was a little annoyed to find Lupin, instead of reading last night, had gone to a common sort of entertainment, given at the Assembly Rooms. I expressed my opinion that such performances were unworthy of respectable patronage; but he replied: 'Oh, it was only "for one night only". I had a fit of the blues come on, and thought I would go to see Polly Presswell, England's Particular Spark.' I told him I was proud to say I had never heard of her. Carrie said: 'Do let the boy alone. He's quite old enough to take care of himself, and won't forget he's a gentleman. Remember, you were young once yourself.' Rained all day hard, but Lupin would go out.

AUGUST 15.—Cleared up a bit, so we all took the train to Margate, and the first person we met on the jetty was Gowing. I said: 'Hulloh! I thought you had gone to Barmouth with your Birmingham friends?' He said: 'Yes, but young Peter Lawrence was so ill, they postponed their visit, so I came down here. You know the Cummings are here too?' Carrie said: 'Oh, that will be delightful! We must have some evenings together and have games.'

I introduced Lupin, saying: 'You will be pleased to find we have our dear boy at home!' Gowing said: 'How's that? You don't mean to say he's left the Bank?'

I changed the subject quickly, and thereby avoided any of those awkward questions which Gowing always has a knack of asking.

AUGUST 16.—Lupin positively refused to walk down the Parade with me because I was wearing my new straw helmet with my frock-coat. I don't know what the boy is coming to.

AUGUST 17.—Lupin not falling in with our views, Carrie and I went for a sail. It was a relief to be with her alone; for when Lupin irritates me, she always sides with him. On our return, he said: 'Oh, you've been on the "Shilling Emetic", have you? You'll come to six-pennorth on the "Liver Jerker" next.' I presume he meant a tricycle, but I affected not to understand him.

AUGUST 18.—Gowing and Cummings walked over to arrange an evening at Margate. It being wet, Gowing asked Cummings to accompany him to the hotel and have a game of billiards, knowing I never play, and in fact disapprove of the game. Cummings said he must hasten back to Margate; whereupon Lupin, to my horror, said: 'I'll give you a game, Gowing—a hundred up. A walk round the cloth will give me an appetite for dinner.' I said: 'Perhaps *Mister* Gowing does not care to play with boys.' Gowing surprised me by saying: 'Oh yes, I do, if they play well,' and they walked off together.

AUGUST 19, SUNDAY.—I was about to read Lupin a sermon on smoking (which he indulges in violently) and billiards, but he put on his hat and walked out. Carrie then read *me* a long sermon on the

'*Lupin positively refused to walk down the Parade with me because I was wearing my new straw helmet with my frock-coat.*'

palpable inadvisability of treating Lupin as if he were a mere child. I felt she was somewhat right, so in the evening I offered him a cigar. He seemed pleased, but, after a few whiffs, said: 'This is a good old tup'ny—try one of mine,' and he handed me a cigar as long as it was strong, which is saying a good deal.

AUGUST 20.—I am glad our last day at the seaside was fine, though clouded overhead. We went over to Cummings' (at Margate) in the evening, and as it was cold, we stayed in and played games; Gowing, as usual, overstepping the mark. He suggested we should play 'Cutlets',* a game we never heard of. He sat on a chair, and asked Carrie to sit on his lap, an invitation which dear Carrie rightly declined.

After some species of wrangling, *I* sat on Gowing's knees and Carrie sat on the edge of mine. Lupin sat on the edge of Carrie's lap, then Cummings on Lupin's, and Mrs Cummings on her husband's. We looked very ridiculous, and laughed a good deal.

Gowing then said: 'Are you a believer in the Great Mogul?' We had to answer all together: 'Yes—oh, yes!' (three times). Gowing said: 'So

*We play the game of 'Cutlets'. When we had all sat on each other's laps, Gowing said:
'Are you a believer in the Great Mogul?'*

Gowing said: 'So am I,' and suddenly got up.

am I,' and suddenly got up. The result of this stupid joke was that we all fell on the ground, and poor Carrie banged her head against the corner of the fender. Mrs Cummings put some vinegar on; but through this we missed the last train, and had to drive back to Broadstairs, which cost me seven-and-sixpence.

CHAPTER VII

Home again. Mrs James' influence on Carrie. Can get nothing for Lupin. Next-door neighbours are a little troublesome. Some one tampers with my diary. Got a place for Lupin. Lupin startles us with an announcement.

AUGUST 22.—Home sweet Home again! Carrie bought some pretty blue-wool mats to stand vases on. Fripps, Janus and Co. write to say they are sorry they have no vacancy among their staff of clerks for Lupin.

AUGUST 23.—I bought a pair of stags' heads made of plaster-of-Paris and coloured brown. They will look just the thing for our little hall, and give it style; the heads are excellent imitations. Poolers and Smith are sorry they have nothing to offer Lupin.

AUGUST 24.—Simply to please Lupin, and make things cheerful for him, as he is a little down, Carrie invited Mrs James to come up from Sutton and spend two or three days with us. We have not said a word to Lupin, but mean to keep it as a surprise.

AUGUST 25.—Mrs James, of Sutton, arrived in the afternoon, bringing with her an enormous bunch of wild flowers. The more I see of Mrs James the nicer I think she is, and she is devoted to Carrie. She went into Carrie's room to take off her bonnet, and remained there nearly an hour talking about dress. Lupin said he was not a bit surprised at Mrs James' *visit*, but was surprised at *her*.

AUGUST 26, SUNDAY.—Nearly late for church, Mrs James having talked considerably about what to wear all the morning. Lupin does not seem to get on very well with Mrs James. I am afraid we shall have some trouble with our next-door neighbours who came in last Wednesday. Several of their friends, who drive up in dog-carts,* have already made themselves objectionable.

An evening or two ago I had put on a white waistcoat for coolness, and while walking past with my thumbs in my waistcoat pockets

*I hung up a stag's head made of
plaster-of-Paris*

(a habit I have), one man, seated in the cart, and looking like an American, commenced singing some vulgar nonsense about '*I had thirteen dollars in my waistcoat pocket.*' I fancied it was meant for me, and my suspicions were confirmed; for while walking round the garden in my tall hat this afternoon, a 'throw-down' cracker was deliberately aimed at my hat, and exploded on it like a percussion cap. I turned sharply, and am positive I saw the man who was in the cart retreating from one of the bedroom windows.

AUGUST 27.—Carrie and Mrs James went off shopping, and had not returned when I came back from the office. Judging from the subsequent conversation, I am afraid Mrs James is filling Carrie's head with a lot of nonsense about dress. I walked over to Gowing's and asked him to drop in to supper, and make things pleasant.

Carrie prepared a little extemporized supper, consisting of the remainder of the cold joint, a small piece of salmon (which I was to refuse, in case there was not enough to go round), and a blancmange and custards. There was also a decanter of port and some jam puffs on the sideboard. Mrs James made us play rather a good game of cards, called 'Muggings'.* To my surprise, in fact disgust, Lupin got up in the middle, and, in a most sarcastic tone, said: 'Pardon me, this sort of thing is too fast for me. I shall go and enjoy a quiet game of marbles in the back-garden.'

Things might have become rather disagreeable but for Gowing (who seems to have taken to Lupin) suggesting they should invent games. Lupin said: 'Let's play "monkeys".' He then led Gowing all round the room, and brought him in front of the looking-glass. I must confess I laughed heartily at this. I was a little vexed at everybody subsequently laughing at some joke which they did not explain, and it was only on going to bed I discovered I must have been walking about all the evening with an antimacassar on one button of my coat-tails.

AUGUST 28.—Found a large brick in the middle bed of geraniums, evidently come from next door. Pattles and Pattles can't find a place for Lupin.

AUGUST 29.—Mrs James is making a positive fool of Carrie. Carrie appeared in a new dress like a smock-frock. She said 'smocking' was all the rage. I replied it put me in a rage. She also had on a hat as big as a kitchen coal-scuttle, and the same shape. Mrs James went home, and both Lupin and I were somewhat pleased—the first time we have agreed on a single subject since his return. Merkins and Son write they have no vacancy for Lupin.

OCTOBER 30.—I should very much like to know who has wilfully torn the last five or six weeks out of my diary. It is perfectly monstrous! Mine is a large scribbling diary, with plenty of space for the record of my everyday events, and in keeping up that record I take (with much pride) a great deal of pains.

I asked Carrie if she knew anything about it. She replied it was my own fault for leaving the diary about with a charwoman cleaning and the sweeps in the house. I said that was not an answer to my question. This retort of mine, which I thought extremely smart, would have been more effective had I not jogged my elbow against a vase on a table temporarily placed in the passage, knocked it over, and smashed it.

Carrie was dreadfully upset at this disaster, for it was one of a pair of vases which cannot be matched, given to us on our wedding-day by Mrs Burtsett, an old friend of Carrie's cousins, the Pommertons, late of Dalston. I called to Sarah, and asked her about the diary. She said she had not been in the sitting-room at all; after the sweep had left, Mrs Birrell (the charwoman) had cleaned the room and lighted the fire herself. Finding a burnt piece of paper in the grate, I examined it, and found it was a piece of my diary. So it was evident some one had torn my diary to light the fire. I requested Mrs Birrell to be sent to me tomorrow.

OCTOBER 31.—Received a letter from our principal, Mr Perkupp, saying that he thinks he knows of a place at last for our dear boy Lupin. This, in a measure, consoles me for the loss of a portion of my diary; for I am bound to confess the last few weeks have been devoted to the record of disappointing answers received from people to whom I have applied for appointments for Lupin. Mrs Birrell called, and, in reply to me, said: 'She never *see* no book, much less take such a liberty as *touch* it.'

I said I was determined to find out who did it, whereupon she said she would do her best to help me; but she remembered the sweep lighting the fire with a bit of the *Echo*. I requested the sweep to be sent to me tomorrow. I wish Carrie had not given Lupin a latch-key; we never seem to see anything of him. I sat up till past one for him, and then retired tired.

NOVEMBER 1.—My entry yesterday about 'retired tired', which I did not notice at the time, is rather funny. If I were not so worried just now, I might have had a little joke about it. The sweep called, but had the audacity to come up to the hall-door and lean his dirty bag of soot on the doorstep. He, however, was so polite, I could not rebuke him. He said Sarah lighted the fire. Unfortunately, Sarah heard this, for she was dusting the banisters, and she ran down, and flew into a temper with the sweep, causing a row on the front doorsteps, which I would not have had happen for anything. I ordered her about her business, and told the sweep I was sorry to have troubled him; and so I was, for the doorsteps were covered with soot in consequence of his visit. I would willingly give ten shillings to find out who tore my diary.

NOVEMBER 2.—I spent the evening quietly with Carrie, of whose company I never tire. We had a most pleasant chat about the letters on 'Is Marriage a Failure?'* It has been no failure in our case. In talking over our own happy experiences, we never noticed that it was past midnight. We were startled by hearing the door slam violently. Lupin had come in. He made no attempt to turn down the gas in the passage, or even to look into the room where we were, but went straight up to bed, making a terrible noise. I asked him to come down for a moment, and he begged to be excused, as he was 'dead beat', an observation that was scarcely consistent with the fact that, for a quarter of an hour afterwards, he was positively dancing in his room, and shouting out, 'See me dance the polka!' or some such nonsense.

NOVEMBER 3.—Good news at last. Mr Perkupp has got an appointment for Lupin, and he is to go and see about it on Monday. Oh, how my mind is relieved! I went to Lupin's room to take the good news to him, but he was in bed, very seedy, so I resolved to keep it over till the evening.

He said he had last night been elected a member of an Amateur Dramatic Club, called the 'Holloway Comedians'; and, though it was a pleasant evening, he had sat in a draught, and got neuralgia in the head. He declined to have any breakfast, so I left him.

In the evening I had up a special bottle of port, and, Lupin being

Mr Perkupp

in for a wonder, we filled our glasses, and I said: 'Lupin my boy, I have some good and unexpected news for you. Mr Perkupp has procured you an appointment!' Lupin said: 'Good biz!' and we drained our glasses.

Lupin then said: 'Fill up the glasses again, for I have some good and unexpected news for you.'

I had some slight misgivings, and so evidently had Carrie, for she said: 'I hope we shall think it good news.'

Lupin said: 'Oh, it's all right! *I'm engaged to be married!*'

Lupin said: '*I'm engaged to be married!*'

CHAPTER VIII

Daisy Mutlar sole topic of conversation. Lupin's new berth. Fireworks at the Cummings'. The 'Holloway Comedians'. Sarah quarrels with the charwoman. Lupin's uncalled-for interference. Am introduced to Daisy Mutlar. We decide to give a party in her honour.

November 5, Sunday.—Carrie and I troubled about that mere boy Lupin getting engaged to be married without consulting us or anything. After dinner he told us all about it. He said the lady's name was Daisy Mutlar, and she was the nicest, prettiest, and most accomplished girl he ever met. He loved her the moment he saw her, and if he had to wait fifty years he would wait, and he knew she would wait for him.

Lupin further said, with much warmth, that the world was a different world to him now—it was a world worth living in. He lived with an object now, and that was to make Daisy Mutlar—Daisy Pooter, and he would guarantee she would not disgrace the family of the Pooters. Carrie here burst out crying, and threw her arms round his neck, and in doing so, upset the glass of port he held in his hand all over his new light trousers.

I said I had no doubt we should like Miss Mutlar when we saw her, but Carrie said she loved her already. I thought this rather premature, but held my tongue. Daisy Mutlar was the sole topic of conversation for the remainder of the day. I asked Lupin who her people were, and he replied: 'Oh, you know Mutlar, Williams and Watts.' I did not know, but refrained from asking any further questions at present, for fear of irritating Lupin.

November 6.—Lupin went with me to the office, and had a long conversation with Mr Perkupp, our principal, the result of which was that he accepted a clerkship in the firm of Job Cleanands and Co., Stock and Share Brokers. Lupin told me, privately, it was an advertising firm, and he did not think much of it. I replied: 'Beggars should not be choosers'; and I will do Lupin the justice to say, he looked rather ashamed of himself.

In the evening we went round to the Cummings', to have a few fireworks. It began to rain, and I thought it rather dull. One of my squibs would not go off, and Gowing said: 'Hit it on your boot, boy; it will go off then.' I gave it a few knocks on the end of my boot, and it went off with one loud explosion, and burnt my fingers rather badly. I gave the rest of the squibs to the little Cummings boy to let off.

Another unfortunate thing happened, which brought a heap of abuse on my head. Cummings fastened a large wheel set-piece on a stake in the ground by way of a grand finale. He made a great fuss about it; said it cost seven shillings. There was a little difficulty in getting it alight. At last it went off; but after a couple of slow revolutions it stopped. I had my stick with me, so I gave it a tap to send it round, and, unfortunately, it fell off the stake on to the grass. Anybody would have thought I had set the house on fire from the way in which they stormed at me. I will never join in any more firework parties. It is a ridiculous waste of time and money.

NOVEMBER 7.—Lupin asked Carrie to call on Mrs Mutlar, but Carrie said she thought Mrs Mutlar ought to call on her first. I agreed with Carrie, and this led to an argument. However, the matter was settled by Carrie saying she could not find any visiting cards, and we must get some more printed, and when they were finished would be quite time enough to discuss the etiquette of calling.

NOVEMBER 8.—I ordered some of our cards at Black's, the stationer's. I ordered twenty-five of each, which will last us for a good long time. In the evening, Lupin brought in Harry Mutlar, Miss Mutlar's brother. He was rather a gawky youth, and Lupin said he was the most popular and best amateur in the club, referring to the 'Holloway Comedians'. Lupin whispered to us that if we could only 'draw out' Harry a bit, he would make us roar with laughter.

At supper, young Mutlar did several amusing things. He took up a knife, and with the flat part of it played a tune on his cheek in a wonderful manner. He also gave an imitation of an old man with no teeth, smoking a big cigar. The way he kept dropping the cigar sent Carrie into fits.

In the course of conversation, Daisy's name cropped up, and young Mutlar said he would bring his sister round to us one evening—his parents being rather old-fashioned, and not going out much. Carrie said we would get up a little special party. As young Mutlar showed no inclination to go, and it was approaching eleven o'clock, as a hint I reminded Lupin that he had to be up early tomorrow. Instead of taking the hint, Mutlar began a series of comic imitations. He went on for an hour without cessation. Poor Carrie could scarcely keep her eyes open. At last she made an excuse, and said 'Good-night'.

Mutlar then left, and I heard him and Lupin whispering in the hall something about the 'Holloway Comedians', and to my disgust, although it was past midnight, Lupin put on his hat and coat, and went out with his new companion.

NOVEMBER 9.—My endeavours to discover who tore the sheets out of my diary still fruitless. Lupin has Daisy Mutlar on the brain, so we see little of him, except that he invariably turns up at meal times. Cummings dropped in.

NOVEMBER 10.—Lupin seems to like his new berth—that's a comfort. Daisy Mutlar the sole topic of conversation during tea. Carrie almost as full of it as Lupin. Lupin informs me, to my disgust, that he has been persuaded to take part in the forthcoming performance of the 'Holloway Comedians'. He says he is to play Bob Britches in the farce, *Gone to my Uncle's*; Frank Mutlar is going to play old Musty. I told Lupin pretty plainly I was not in the least degree interested in the matter, and totally disapproved of amateur theatricals. Gowing came in the evening.

NOVEMBER 11.—Returned home to find the house in a most disgraceful uproar. Carrie, who appeared very frightened, was standing outside her bedroom, while Sarah was excited and crying. Mrs Birrell (the charwoman), who had evidently been drinking, was shouting at the top of her voice that she was 'no thief, that she was a respectable woman, who had to work hard for her living, and she would smack anyone's face who put lies into her mouth'. Lupin, whose back was towards me, did not hear me come in. He was standing between the two women, and, I regret to say, in his endeavour to act as peacemaker, he made use of rather strong language in the presence of his mother; and I was just in time to hear him say: 'And all this fuss about the loss of a few pages from a rotten diary that wouldn't fetch three-halfpence a pound!' I said, quietly: 'Pardon me, Lupin, that is a matter of opinion; and as I am master of this house, perhaps you will allow me to take the reins.'

I ascertained that the cause of the row was, that Sarah had accused Mrs Birrell of tearing the pages out of my diary to wrap up some kitchen fat and leavings which she had taken out of the house last week. Mrs Birrell had slapped Sarah's face, and said she had taken nothing out of the place, as there was 'never no leavings to take'. I ordered Sarah back to her work, and requested Mrs Birrell to go home. When I entered the parlour Lupin was kicking his legs in the air, and roaring with laughter.

NOVEMBER 12, SUNDAY.—Coming home from church Carrie and I met Lupin, Daisy Mutlar, and her brother. Daisy was introduced to us, and we walked home together, Carrie walking on with Miss Mutlar. We asked them in for a few minutes, and I had a good look at my future daughter-in-law. My heart quite sank. She is a big young woman, and I should think at least eight years older than Lupin. I did not even think her good-looking. Carrie asked her if she could come in on Wednesday next with her brother to meet a few friends. She replied that she would only be too pleased.

NOVEMBER 13.—Carrie sent out invitations to Gowing, the Cummings, to Mr and Mrs James (of Sutton), and Mr Stillbrook. I wrote a note to Mr Franching, of Peckham. Carrie said we may as well make it a nice affair, and why not ask our principal, Mr Perkupp? I said I feared we were not quite grand enough for him. Carrie said there was 'no offence in asking him'. I said: 'Certainly not,' and I wrote him a letter. Carrie confessed she was a little disappointed with Daisy Mutlar's appearance, but thought she seemed a nice girl.

NOVEMBER 14.—Everybody so far has accepted for our quite grand little party for tomorrow. Mr Perkupp, in a nice letter which I shall keep, wrote that he was dining in Kensington, but if he could get away, he would come up to Holloway for an hour. Carrie was busy all day, making little cakes and open jam puffs and jellies. She said she felt quite nervous about her responsibilities tomorrow evening. We decided to have some light things on the table, such as sandwiches,

Daisy Mutlar

cold chicken and ham, and some sweets, and on the sideboard a nice piece of cold beef and a Paysandu tongue* for the more hungry ones to peg into if they liked.

Gowing called to know if he was to put on 'swallow-tails' tomorrow. Carrie said he had better dress, especially as Mr Franching was coming, and there was a possibility of Mr Perkupp also putting in an appearance.

Gowing said: 'Oh, I only wanted to know; for I have not worn my dress-coat for some time, and I must send it to have the creases pressed out.'

After Gowing left, Lupin came in, and in his anxiety to please Daisy Mutlar, carped at and criticized the arrangements, and, in fact, disapproved of everything, including our having asked our old friend Cummings, who, he said, would look in evening-dress like a green-grocer engaged to wait, and who must not be surprised if Daisy took him for one.

I fairly lost my temper, and said: 'Lupin, allow me to tell you Miss Daisy Mutlar is not the Queen of England. I gave you credit for more wisdom than to allow yourself to be inveigled into an engagement with a woman considerably older than yourself. I advise you to think of earning your living before entangling yourself with a wife whom you will have to support, and, in all probability, her brother also, who appeared to be nothing but a loafer.'

Instead of receiving this advice in a sensible manner, Lupin jumped up and said: 'If you insult the lady I am engaged to, you insult me. I will leave the house and never darken your doors again.'

He went out of the house, slamming the hall-door. But it was all right. He came back to supper, and we played Bézique till nearly twelve o'clock.

CHAPTER IX

Our first important Party. Old Friends and New Friends. Gowing is a little annoying; but his friend, Mr Stillbrook, turns out to be quite amusing. Inopportune arrival of Mr Perkupp, but he is most kind and complimentary. Party a great success.

NOVEMBER 15.—A red-letter day. Our first important party since we have been in this house. I got home early from the City. Lupin insisted on having a hired waiter, and stood a half-dozen of champagne. I think this an unnecessary expense, but Lupin said he had had a piece of luck, having made three pounds out of a private deal in the City. I hope he won't gamble in his new situation. The supper-room looked so nice, and Carrie truly said: 'We need not be ashamed of its being seen by Mr Perkupp, should he honour us by coming.'

I dressed early in case people should arrive punctually at eight o'clock, and was much vexed to find my new dress-trousers much too short. Lupin, who is getting beyond his position, found fault with my wearing ordinary boots instead of dress-boots.

I replied satirically: 'My dear son, I have lived to be above that sort of thing.'

Lupin burst out laughing, and said: 'A man generally was above his boots.'

This may be funny, or it may *not*; but I was gratified to find he had not discovered the coral had come off one of my studs. Carrie looked a picture, wearing the dress she wore at the Mansion House. The arrangement of the drawing-room was excellent. Carrie had hung muslin curtains over the folding-doors, and also over one of the entrances, for we had removed the door from its hinges.

Mr Peters, the waiter, arrived in good time, and I gave him strict orders not to open another bottle of champagne until the previous one was empty. Carrie arranged for some sherry and port wine to be placed on the drawing-room sideboard, with some glasses. By-the-by, our new enlarged and tinted photographs look very nice on the walls, especially as Carrie has arranged some Liberty silk bows on the four corners of them.

The first arrival was Gowing, who, with his usual taste, greeted me with: 'Hulloh, Pooter, why your trousers are too short!'

I simply said: 'Very likely, and you will find my temper "*short*" also.'

He said: 'That won't make your trousers longer, Juggins. You should get your missus to put a flounce on them.'

I wonder I waste my time entering his insulting observations in my diary.

The next arrivals were Mr and Mrs Cummings. The former said: 'As you didn't say anything about dress, I have come "half dress".' He had on a black frock-coat and white tie. The James', Mr Merton, and Mr Stillbrook arrived, but Lupin was restless and unbearable till his Daisy Mutlar and Frank arrived.

Carrie and I were rather startled at Daisy's appearance. She had a bright-crimson dress on, cut very low in the neck. I do not think such a style modest. She ought to have taken a lesson from Carrie, and covered her shoulders with a little lace. Mr Nackles, Mr Sprice-Hogg and his four daughters came; so did Franching, and one or two of Lupin's new friends, members of the 'Holloway Comedians'. Some of these seemed rather theatrical in their manner, especially one, who was posing all the evening, and leant on our little round table and cracked it. Lupin called him 'our Henry', and said he was 'our lead at the H.C.'s', and was quite as good in that department as Harry Mutlar was as the low-comedy merchant. All this is Greek to me.

We had some music, and Lupin, who never left Daisy's side for a moment, raved over her singing of a song, called 'Some Day'.* It seemed a pretty song, but she made such grimaces, and sang, to my mind, so out of tune, I would not have asked her to sing again; but Lupin made her sing four songs right off, one after the other.

At ten o'clock we went down to supper, and from the way Gowing and Cummings ate you would have thought they had not had a meal for a month. I told Carrie to keep something back in case Mr Perkupp should come by mere chance. Gowing annoyed me very much by filling a large tumbler of champagne, and drinking it straight off. He repeated this action, and made me fear our half-dozen of champagne would not last out. I tried to keep a bottle back, but

Lupin got hold of it, and took it to the side-table with Daisy and Frank Mutlar.

We went upstairs, and the young fellows began skylarking. Carrie put a stop to that at once. Stillbrook amused us with a song, 'What have you done with your Cousin John?' I did not notice that Lupin and Frank had disappeared. I asked Mr Watson, one of the Holloways, where they were, and he said: 'It's a case of "Oh, what a surprise!"'

We were directed to form a circle—which we did. Watson then said: 'I have much pleasure in introducing the celebrated Blondin* Donkey.' Frank and Lupin then bounded into the room. Lupin had whitened his face like a clown, and Frank had tied round his waist a large hearthrug. He was supposed to be the donkey, and he looked it. They indulged in a very noisy pantomime, and we were all shrieking with laughter.

I turned round suddenly, and then I saw Mr Perkupp standing half-way in the door, he having arrived without our knowing it. I beckoned to Carrie, and we went up to him at once. He would not come right into the room. I apologized for the foolery, but Mr Perkupp said: 'Oh, it seems amusing.' I could see he was not a bit amused.

Carrie and I took him downstairs, but the table was a wreck. There was not a glass of champagne left—not even a sandwich. Mr Perkupp said he required nothing, but would like a glass of seltzer or soda water. The last syphon was empty. Carrie said: 'We have plenty of port wine left.' Mr Perkupp said, with a smile: 'No, thank you. I really require nothing, but I am most pleased to see you and your husband in your own home. Good-night, Mrs Pooter—you will excuse my very short stay, I know.' I went with him to his carriage, and he said: 'Don't trouble to come to the office till twelve tomorrow.'

I felt despondent as I went back to the house, and I told Carrie I thought the party was a failure. Carrie said it was a great success, and I was only tired, and insisted on my having some port myself. I drank two glasses, and felt much better, and we went into the drawing-room, where they had commenced dancing. Carrie and I had a little dance, which I said reminded me of old days. She said I was a spooney old thing.

CHAPTER X

Reflections. I make another Good Joke. Am annoyed at the constant serving-up of the 'Blancmange'. Lupin expresses his opinion of Weddings. Lupin falls out with Daisy Mutlar.

NOVEMBER 16.—Woke about twenty times during the night, with terrible thirst. Finished off all the water in the bottle, as well as half that in the jug. Kept dreaming also, that last night's party was a failure, and that a lot of low people came without invitation, and kept chaffing and throwing things at Mr Perkupp, till at last I was obliged to hide him in the box-room (which we had just discovered), with a bath-towel over him. It seems absurd now, but it was painfully real in the dream. I had the same dream about a dozen times.

Carrie annoyed me by saying: 'You know champagne never agrees with you.' I told her I had only a couple of glasses of it, having kept myself entirely to port. I added that good champagne hurt nobody, and Lupin told me he had only got it from a traveller as a favour, as that particular brand had been entirely bought up by a West-End club.

I think I ate too heartily of the 'side dishes', as the waiter called them. I said to Carrie: 'I wish I had put those "side dishes" *aside*.' I repeated this, but Carrie was busy, packing up the teaspoons we had borrowed of Mrs Cummings for the party. It was just half-past eleven, and I was starting for the office, when Lupin appeared, with a yellow complexion, and said: 'Hulloh! Guv., what priced head have you this morning?' I told him he might just as well speak to me in Dutch. He added: 'When I woke this morning, my head was as big as Baldwin's balloon.'* On the spur of the moment I said the cleverest thing I think I have ever said; viz.: 'Perhaps that accounts for the para*shooting* pains.' We all three roared.

NOVEMBER 17.—Still feel tired and headachy! In the evening Gowing called, and was full of praise about our party last Wednesday. He said everything was done beautifully, and he enjoyed himself enormously. Gowing can be a very nice fellow when he likes, but you never know how long it will last. For instance, he stopped to supper, and seeing some blancmange on the table, shouted out, while the servant was in the room: 'Hulloh! The remains of Wednesday?'

NOVEMBER 18.—Woke up quite fresh after a good night's rest, and feel quite myself again. I am satisfied a life of going-out and Society is not a life for me; we therefore declined the invitation which we received this morning to Miss Bird's wedding. We only met her twice at Mrs James', and it means a present. Lupin said: 'I am with you for once. To my mind a wedding's a very poor play. There are only two parts in it—the bride and bridegroom. The best man is only a walking gentleman. With the exception of a crying father and a snivelling mother, the rest are *supers* who have to dress well and have to *pay* for their insignificant parts in the shape of costly presents.' I did not care for the theatrical slang, but thought it clever, though disrespectful.

I told Sarah not to bring up the blancmange again for breakfast. It seems to have been placed on our table at every meal since Wednesday. Cummings came round in the evening, and congratulated us on the success of our party. He said it was the best party he had been to for many a year; but he wished we had let him know it was full dress, as he would have turned up in his swallow-tails. We sat down to a quiet game of dominoes, and were interrupted by the noisy entrance of Lupin and Frank Mutlar. Cummings and I asked them to join us. Lupin said he did not care for dominoes, and suggested a game of 'Spoof'. On my asking if it required counters, Frank and Lupin in measured time said: 'One, two, three; go! Have you an estate in Greenland?' It was simply Greek to me, but it appears it is one of the customs of the 'Holloway Comedians' to do this when a member displays ignorance.

In spite of my instructions, that blancmange was brought up again for supper. To make matters worse, there had been an attempt to disguise it, by placing it in a glass dish with jam round it. Carrie asked Lupin if he would have some, and he replied: 'No second-hand goods for me, thank you.' I told Carrie, when we were alone, if that blanc-mange were placed on the table again I should walk out of the house.

NOVEMBER 19, SUNDAY.—A delightfully quiet day. In the afternoon Lupin was off to spend the rest of the day with the Mutlars. He departed in the best of spirits, and Carrie said: 'Well, one advantage of Lupin's engagement with Daisy is that the boy seems happy all day long. That quite reconciles me to what I must confess seems an imprudent engagement.'

Carrie and I talked the matter over during the evening, and agreed that it did not always follow that an early engagement meant an unhappy marriage. Dear Carrie reminded me that we married early, and, with the exception of a few trivial misunderstandings, we had never had a really serious word. I could not help thinking (as I told her) that half the pleasures of life were derived from the little struggles and small privations that one had to endure at the beginning of one's married life. Such struggles were generally occasioned by want of means, and often helped to make loving couples stand together all the firmer.

Carrie said I had expressed myself wonderfully well, and that I was quite a philosopher.

We are all vain at times, and I must confess I felt flattered by Carrie's little compliment. I don't pretend to be able to express myself in fine language, but I feel I have the power of expressing my thoughts with simplicity and lucidness. About nine o'clock, to our surprise, Lupin entered, with a wild, reckless look, and in a hollow voice, which I must say seemed rather theatrical, said: 'Have you any brandy?' I said: 'No; but here is some whisky.' Lupin drank off nearly a wineglassful without water, to my horror.

We all three sat reading in silence till ten, when Carrie and I rose to go to bed. Carrie said to Lupin: 'I hope Daisy is well?'

Lupin, with a forced careless air that he must have picked up from the 'Holloway Comedians', replied: 'Oh, Daisy? You mean Miss Mutlar. I don't know whether she is well or not, but please *never to mention her name again in my presence.*'

CHAPTER XI

We have a dose of Irving imitations. Make the acquaintance of a Mr Padge. Don't care for him. Mr Burwin-Fosselton becomes a nuisance.

NOVEMBER 20.—Have seen nothing of Lupin the whole day. Bought a cheap address-book. I spent the evening copying in the names and addresses of my friends and acquaintances. Left out the Mutlars of course.

NOVEMBER 21.—Lupin turned up for a few minutes in the evening. He asked for a drop of brandy with a sort of careless look, which to my mind was theatrical and quite ineffective. I said: 'My boy, I have none, and I don't think I should give it you if I had.' Lupin said: 'I'll go where I can get some,' and walked out of the house. Carrie took the boy's part, and the rest of the evening was spent in a disagreeable discussion, in which the words 'Daisy' and 'Mutlar' must have occurred a thousand times.

NOVEMBER 22.—Gowing and Cummings dropped in during the evening. Lupin also came in, bringing his friend, Mr Burwin-Fosselton*—one of the 'Holloway Comedians'—who was at our party the other night, and who cracked our little round table. Happy to say Daisy Mutlar was never referred to. The conversation was almost entirely monopolized by the young fellow Fosselton, who not only looked rather like Mr Irving,* but seemed to imagine that he *was* the celebrated actor. I must say he gave some capital imitations of him. As he showed no signs of moving at supper time, I said: 'If you like to stay, Mr Fosselton, for our usual crust—pray do.' He replied: 'Oh! thanks; but please call me Burwin-Fosselton. It is a double name. There are lots of Fosseltons, but please call me Burwin-Fosselton.'

He began doing the Irving business all through supper. He sank so low down in his chair that his chin was almost on a level with the table, and twice he kicked Carrie under the table, upset his wine, and flashed a knife uncomfortably near Gowing's face. After supper he kept stretching out his legs on the fender, indulging in scraps of

Mr Burwin-Fosselton at supper.

quotations from plays which were Greek to me, and more than once knocked over the fire-irons, making a hideous row—poor Carrie already having a bad headache.

When he went, he said, to our surprise: 'I will come tomorrow and bring my Irving make-up.' Gowing and Cummings said they would like to see it and would come too. I could not help thinking they might as well give a party at my house while they are about it. However, as Carrie sensibly said: 'Do anything, dear, to make Lupin forget the Daisy Mutlar business.'

NOVEMBER 23.—In the evening, Cummings came early. Gowing came a little later and brought, without asking permission, a fat and, I think, very vulgar-looking man named Padge, who appeared to be all moustache. Gowing never attempted any apology to either of us, but said Padge wanted to see the Irving business, to which Padge said: 'That's right,' and that is about all he *did* say during the entire evening. Lupin came in and seemed in much better spirits. He had prepared a bit of a surprise. Mr Burwin-Fosselton had come in with him, but had gone upstairs to get ready. In half-an-hour Lupin retired from the parlour, and returning in a few minutes, announced 'Mr Henry Irving'.

I must say we were all astounded. I never saw such a resemblance. It was astonishing. The only person who did not appear interested was the man. Padge, who had got the best armchair, and was puffing away at a foul pipe into the fireplace. After some little time I said: 'Why do actors always wear their hair so long?' Carrie in a moment said, 'Mr Hare* doesn't wear long *hair*.' How we laughed except Mr Fosselton, who said, in a rather patronizing kind of way, 'The joke, Mrs Pooter, is extremely appropriate, if not altogether new.' Thinking this rather a snub, I said: 'Mr Fosselton, I fancy——' He interrupted me by saying: 'Mr *Burwin*-Fosselton, if you please,' which made me quite forget what I was going to say to him. During the supper Mr Burwin-Fosselton again monopolized the conversation with his Irving talk, and both Carrie and I came to the conclusion one can have even too much imitation of Irving. After supper, Mr Burwin-Fosselton got a little too boisterous over his Irving imitation, and suddenly seizing Gowing by the collar of his coat, dug his thumb-nail, accidentally of course, into Gowing's neck and took a piece of flesh out. Gowing was rightly annoyed, but that man Padge, who having

Mr Padge

declined our modest supper in order that he should not lose his comfortable chair, burst into an uncontrollable fit of laughter at the little misadventure. I was so annoyed at the conduct of Padge, I said: 'I suppose you would have laughed if he had poked Mr Gowing's eye out?' to which Padge replied: 'That's right,' and laughed more than ever. I think perhaps the greatest surprise was when we broke up, for Mr Burwin-Fosselton said: 'Good-night, Mr Pooter. I'm glad you like the imitation, I'll bring *the other make-up tomorrow night.*'

NOVEMBER 24.—I went to town without a pocket-handkerchief. This is the second time I have done this during the last week. I must be losing my memory. Had it not been for this Daisy Mutlar business, I would have written to Mr Burwin-Fosselton and told him I should be *out* this evening, but I fancy he is the sort of young man who would come all the same.

Lupin announces 'Mr Henry Irving'.

Dear old Cummings came in the evening; but Gowing sent round a little note saying he hoped I would excuse his not turning up, which rather amused me. He added that his neck was still painful. Of course, Burwin-Fosselton came, but Lupin never turned up, and imagine my utter disgust when that man Padge actually came again, and not even accompanied by Gowing. I was exasperated, and said: 'Mr Padge, this is a *surprise*.' Dear Carrie, fearing unpleasantness, said: 'Oh! I suppose Mr Padge has only come to see the other Irving make-up.' Mr Padge said: 'That's right,' and took the best chair again, from which he never moved the whole evening.

My only consolation is, he takes no supper, so he is not an expensive guest, but I shall speak to Gowing about the matter. The Irving imitations and conversations occupied the whole evening, till I was sick of it. Once we had a rather heated discussion, which was commenced by Cummings saying that it appeared to him that Mr Burwin-Fosselton was not only *like* Mr Irving, but was in his judgement every way as *good* or even *better*. I ventured to remark that after all it was but an imitation of an original.

Cummings said surely some imitations were better than the originals. I made what I considered a very clever remark: 'Without an original there can be no imitation.' Mr Burwin-Fosselton said quite impertinently: 'Don't discuss me in my presence, if you please; and, Mr Pooter, I should advise you to talk about what you understand'; to which that cad Padge replied: 'That's right.' Dear Carrie saved the whole thing by suddenly saying: 'I'll be Ellen Terry.'* Dear Carrie's imitation wasn't a bit liked, but she was so spontaneous and so funny that the disagreeable discussion passed off. When they left, I very pointedly said to Mr Burwin-Fosselton and Mr Padge that we should be engaged tomorrow evening.

NOVEMBER 25.—Had a long letter from Mr Fosselton respecting last night's Irving discussion. I was very angry, and I wrote and said I knew little or nothing about stage matters, was not in the least interested in them and positively declined to be drawn into a discussion on the subject, even at the risk of its leading to a breach of friendship. I never wrote a more determined letter.

On returning home at the usual hour on Saturday afternoon I met near the Archway Daisy Mutlar. My heart gave a leap. I bowed rather stiffly, but she affected not to have seen me. Very much annoyed in the evening by the laundress sending home an odd sock. Sarah said she sent two pairs, and the laundress declared only a pair and a half were sent. I spoke to Carrie about it, but she rather testily replied: 'I am tired of speaking to her; you had better go and speak to her yourself. She is outside.' I did so, but the laundress declared that only an odd sock was sent.

Gowing passed into the passage at this time and was rude enough to listen to the conversation, and interrupting, said: 'Don't waste the odd sock, old man; do an act of charity and give it to some poor man with only one leg.' The laundress giggled like an idiot. I was disgusted and walked upstairs for the purpose of pinning down my collar, as the button had come off the back of my shirt.

When I returned to the parlour, Gowing was retailing his idiotic joke about the odd sock, and Carrie was roaring with laughter. I suppose I am losing my sense of humour. I spoke my mind pretty freely about Padge. Gowing said he had met him only once before that evening. He had been introduced by a friend, and as he (Padge) had 'stood' a good dinner, Gowing wished to show him some little return. Upon my word, Gowing's coolness surpasses all belief. Lupin came in before I could reply, and Gowing unfortunately inquired after Daisy Mutlar. Lupin shouted: 'Mind your own business, sir!' and bounced out of the room, slamming the door. The remainder of the night was Daisy Mutlar—Daisy Mutlar—Daisy Mutlar. Oh dear!

NOVEMBER 26, SUNDAY.—The curate preached a very good sermon today—very good indeed. His appearance is never so impressive as our dear old vicar's, but I am bound to say his sermons are much more impressive. A rather annoying incident occurred, of which I must make mention. Mrs Fernlosse, who is quite a grand lady, living in one of those large houses in the Camden Road, stopped to speak to me after church, when we were all coming out. I must say I felt flattered, for she is thought a good deal of. I suppose she knew me through seeing me so often take round the plate, especially as she always occupies the corner seat of the pew. She is a very influential lady, and may have had something of the utmost importance to say, but unfortunately, as she commenced to speak a strong gust of wind came and blew my hat off into the middle of the road.

I had to run after it, and had the greatest difficulty in recovering it. When I had succeeded in doing so, I found Mrs Fernlosse had walked on with some swell friends, and I felt I could not well approach her now, especially as my hat was smothered with mud. I cannot say how disappointed I felt.

In the evening (*Sunday* evening of all others) I found an impertinent note from Mr Burwin-Fosselton, which ran as follows:

'DEAR MR POOTER, Although your junior by perhaps some twenty or thirty years—which is sufficient reason that you ought to have a longer record of the things and ways in this miniature of a planet—I feel it is just within the bounds of possibility that the wheels of *your* life don't travel so quickly round as those of the humble writer of these lines. The dandy horse* of past days has been known to overtake the *slow coach*.

Do I make myself understood?

Very well, then! Permit me, Mr Pooter, to advise you to accept the *verb. sap.** Acknowledge your defeat, and take your whipping gracefully; for remember *you* threw down the glove, and I cannot claim to be either mentally or physically a *coward*!

Revenons à nos moutons.*

Our lives run in different grooves. I live for MY ART—THE STAGE. Your life is devoted to commercial pursuits—'A life among Ledgers.' My books are of different metal. Your life in the City is honourable, I admit. *But how different!* Cannot even you see the ocean between us? A channel that prevents the meeting of our brains in harmonious accord. Ah! But *chacun à son goût*.*

I have registered a vow to mount the steps of fame. I may crawl, I may slip, I may even falter (we are all weak), but *reach the top rung of the ladder I will!!!!* When there, my voice shall be heard, for I will shout to the multitudes below: '*Vici!*'* For the present I am only an amateur, and my work is unknown, forsooth, save to a party of friends, with here and there an enemy.

But, Mr Pooter, let me ask you, 'What is the difference between the amateur and the professional?'

None!!!

Stay! Yes, there is a difference. One is *paid* for doing what the other does as skilfully for *nothing*!

But *I* will be *paid*, too! For *I*, contrary to the wishes of my family and friends, have at last elected to adopt the stage as *my* profession. And when the *farce* craze is over—*and, mark you, that will be soon*—I will make my power known; for I feel—pardon my apparent conceit—that there is no living man who can play the hump-backed Richard* as I *feel* and *know* I can.

And *you* will be the first to come round and bend your head in submission. There are many matters you may understand, but knowledge of the fine art of acting is to you an *unknown quantity*.

Pray let this discussion cease with this letter. *Vale!**

Yours truly,

BURWIN-FOSSELTON.

I was disgusted. When Lupin came in, I handed him this impertinent letter, and said: 'My boy, in that letter you can see the true character of your friend.'

Lupin, to my surprise, said: 'Oh yes. He showed me the letter before he sent it. I think he is right, and you ought to apologize.'

CHAPTER XII

A serious discussion concerning the use and value of my diary. Lupin's opinion of 'Xmas. Lupin's unfortunate engagement is on again.

DECEMBER 17.—As I open my scribbling diary I find the words 'Oxford Michaelmas Term* ends'. Why this should induce me to indulge in retrospective I don't know, but it does. The last few weeks of my diary are of minimum interest. The breaking off of the engagement between Lupin and Daisy Mutlar has made him a different being, and Carrie a rather depressing companion. She was a little dull last Saturday, and I thought to cheer her up by reading some extracts from my diary; but she walked out of the room in the middle of the reading, without a word. On her return, I said: 'Did my diary bore you, darling?'

She replied, to my surprise: 'I really wasn't listening, dear. I was obliged to leave to give instructions to the laundress. In consequence of some stuff she puts in the water, two more of Lupin's coloured shirts have run; and he says he won't wear them.'

I said: 'Everything is Lupin. It's all Lupin, Lupin, Lupin. There was not a single button on *my* shirt yesterday, but *I* made no complaint.'

Carrie simply replied: 'You should do as all other men do, and wear studs. In fact, I never saw anyone but you wear buttons on the shirt-fronts.'

I said: 'I certainly wore none yesterday, for there were none on.'

Another thought that strikes me is that Gowing seldom calls in the evening, and Cummings never does. I fear they don't get on well with Lupin.

DECEMBER 18.—Yesterday I was in a retrospective vein—today it is *prospective*. I see nothing but clouds, clouds, clouds. Lupin is perfectly intolerable over the Daisy Mutlar business. He won't say what is the cause of the breach. He is evidently condemning her conduct, and yet, if we venture to agree with him, says he won't hear a word against her. So what is one to do? Another thing which is disappointing to me is, that Carrie and Lupin take no interest whatever in my diary.

I broached the subject at the breakfast-table today. I said: 'I was in hopes that, if anything ever happened to me, the diary would be an endless source of pleasure to you both; to say nothing of the chance of the remuneration which may accrue from its being published.'

Both Carrie and Lupin burst out laughing. Carrie was sorry for this, I could see, for she said: 'I did not mean to be rude, dear Charlie; but *truly* I do not think your diary would sufficiently interest the public to be taken up by a publisher.'

I replied: 'I am sure it would prove quite as interesting as some of the ridiculous reminiscences that have been published lately. Besides, it's the diary that makes the man. Where would Evelyn and Pepys* have been if it had not been for their diaries?'

Carrie said I was quite a philosopher; but Lupin, in a jeering tone, said: 'If it had been written on larger paper, Guv., we might get a fair price from a butterman for it.'

As I am in the prospective vein, I vow the end of this year will see the end of my diary.

DECEMBER 19.—The annual invitation came to spend Christmas with Carrie's mother—the usual family festive gathering to which we always look forward. Lupin declined to go. I was astounded, and expressed my surprise and disgust. Lupin then obliged us with the following Radical speech: 'I hate a family gathering at Christmas. What does it mean? Why, someone says: "Ah! we miss poor Uncle James, who was here last year," and we all begin to snivel. Someone else says: "It's two years since poor Aunt Liz used to sit in that corner." Then we all begin to snivel again. Then another gloomy relation says: "Ah! I wonder whose turn it will be next?" Then we all snivel again, and proceed to eat and drink too much; and they don't discover until *I* get up that we have been seated thirteen at dinner.'*

DECEMBER 20.—Went to Smirksons', the drapers, in the Strand, who this year have turned out everything in the shop and devoted the whole place to the sale of Christmas cards. Shop crowded with people, who seemed to take up the cards rather roughly, and, after a hurried glance at them, throw them down again. I remarked to one of the young persons serving, that carelessness appeared to be a disease with some purchasers. The observation was scarcely out of my mouth, when my thick coat-sleeve caught against a large pile of expensive cards in boxes one on top of the other, and threw them down. The manager came forward, looking very much annoyed, and picking up several cards from the ground, said to one of the assistants, with a palpable side-glance at me: 'Put these amongst the sixpenny goods; they can't be sold for a shilling now.' The result was, I felt it my duty to buy some of these damaged cards.

I had to buy more and pay more than intended. Unfortunately I did not examine them all, and when I got home I discovered a vulgar card with a picture of a fat nurse with two babies, one black and the other white, and the words: 'We wish Pa a Merry Christmas.' I tore up the card and threw it away. Carrie said the great disadvantage of going out in Society and increasing the number of our friends was, that we should have to send out nearly two dozen cards this year.

DECEMBER 21.—To save the postman a miserable Christmas, we follow the example of all unselfish people, and send out our cards early. Most of the cards had finger-marks, which I did not notice at night. I shall buy all future cards in the daytime. Lupin (who, ever since he has had the appointment with a stock and share broker, does not seem over-scrupulous in his dealings) told me never to rub out the pencilled price on the backs of the cards. I asked him why. Lupin said: 'Suppose your card is marked 9*d*. Well, all you have to do is to pencil a 3—and a long down-stroke after it—in *front* of the ninepence, and people will think you have given five times the price for it.'

In the evening Lupin was very low-spirited, and I reminded him that behind the clouds the sun was shining. He said: 'Ugh! it never shines on me.' I said: 'Stop, Lupin, my boy; you are worried about Daisy Mutlar. Don't think of her any more. You ought to congratulate yourself on having got off a very bad bargain. Her notions are far too grand for our simple tastes.' He jumped up and said: 'I won't allow one word to be uttered against her. She's worth the whole bunch of your friends put together, that inflated, sloping-head of a Perkupp included.' I left the room with silent dignity, but caught my foot in the mat.

DECEMBER 23.—I exchanged no words with Lupin in the morning; but as he seemed to be in exuberant spirits in the evening, I ventured to ask him where he intended to spend his Christmas. He replied: 'Oh, most likely at the Mutlars.'

In wonderment, I said: 'What! after your engagement has been broken off?'

Lupin said: 'Who said it is off?'

I said: 'You have given us both to understand——'

He interrupted me by saying: 'Well, never mind what I said. *It is on again—there!*'

CHAPTER XIII

*I receive an insulting Christmas card. We spend a pleasant Christmas at
Carrie's mother's. A Mr Moss is rather too free. A boisterous evening,
during which I am struck in the dark. I receive an extraordinary letter
from Mr Mutlar, senior, respecting Lupin. We miss drinking out the Old
Year.*

DECEMBER 24.—I am a poor man, but I would gladly give ten shillings
to find out who sent me the insulting Christmas card I received this
morning. I never insult people; why should they insult me? The worst
part of the transaction is, that I find myself suspecting all my friends.
The handwriting on the envelope is evidently disguised, being written sloping the wrong way. I cannot think either Gowing or
Cummings would do such a mean thing. Lupin denied all knowledge
of it, and I believe him; although I disapprove of his laughing and
sympathizing with the offender. Mr Franching would be above such
an act; and I don't think any of the Mutlars would descend to such a
course. I wonder if Pitt, that impudent clerk at the office, did it? Or
Mrs Birrell, the charwoman, or Burwin-Fosselton? The writing is too
good for the former.

CHRISTMAS DAY.—We caught the 10.20 train at Paddington, and
spent a pleasant day at Carrie's mother's. The country was quite nice
and pleasant, although the roads were sloppy.* We dined in the
middle of the day, just ten of us, and talked over old times. If
everybody had a nice, *un*interfering mother-in-law, such as I have,
what a deal of happiness there would be in the world. Being all in
good spirits, I proposed her health; and I made, I think, a very good
speech.

I concluded, rather neatly, by saying: 'On an occasion like this—
whether relatives, friends, or acquaintances—we are all inspired with
good feelings towards each other. We are of one mind, and think only
of love and friendship. Those who have quarrelled with absent
friends should kiss and make it up. Those who happily have *not* fallen
out, can kiss all the same.'

I saw the tears in the eyes of both Carrie and her mother, and must say I felt very flattered by the compliment. That dear old Reverend John Panzy Smith, who married us, made a most cheerful and amusing speech, and said he should act on my suggestion respecting the kissing. He then walked round the table and kissed all the ladies, including Carrie. Of course one did not object to this; but I was more than staggered when a young fellow named Moss, who was a stranger to me, and who had scarcely spoken a word through dinner, jumped up suddenly with a sprig of mistletoe, and exclaimed: 'Hulloh! I don't see why I shouldn't be on in this scene.' Before one could realize what he was about to do, he kissed Carrie and the rest of the ladies.

Fortunately the matter was treated as a joke, and we all laughed; but it was a dangerous experiment, and I felt very uneasy for a moment as to the result. I subsequently referred to the matter to Carrie, but she said: 'Oh, he's not much more than a boy.' I said that he had a very large moustache for a boy. Carrie replied: 'I didn't say he was not a nice boy.'

DECEMBER 26.—I did not sleep very well last night; I never do in a strange bed. I feel a little indigestion, which one must expect at this time of the year. Carrie and I returned to Town in the evening. Lupin came in late. He said he enjoyed his Christmas, and added: 'I feel as fit as a Lowther Arcade* fiddle, and only require a little more "oof" to feel as fit as a £500 Stradivarius.'* I have long since given up trying to understand Lupin's slang, or asking him to explain it.

DECEMBER 27.—I told Lupin I was expecting Gowing and Cummings to drop in tomorrow evening for a quiet game. I was in hope the boy would volunteer to stay in, and help to amuse them. Instead of which, he said: 'Oh, you had better put them off, as I have asked Daisy and Frank Mutlar to come.' I said I could not think of doing such a thing. Lupin said: 'Then I will send a wire, and put off Daisy.' I suggested that a postcard or letter would reach her quite soon enough, and would not be so extravagant.

Carrie, who had listened to the above conversation with apparent annoyance, directed a well-aimed shaft at Lupin. She said: 'Lupin, why do you object to Daisy meeting your father's friends? Is it because they are not good enough for her, or (which is equally possible) *she* is not good enough for them?' Lupin was dumbfounded, and could make no reply. When he left the room, I gave Carrie a kiss of approval.

DECEMBER 28.—Lupin, on coming down to breakfast, said to his mother: 'I have not put off Daisy and Frank, and should like them to join Gowing and Cummings this evening.' I felt very pleased with the boy for this. Carrie said, in reply: 'I am glad you let me know in time, as I can turn over the cold leg of mutton, dress it with a little parsley, and no one will know it has been cut.' She further said she would make a few custards, and stew some pippins, so that they would be cold by the evening.

Finding Lupin in good spirits, I asked him quietly if he really had any personal objection to either Gowing or Cummings. He replied: 'Not in the least. I think Cummings looks rather an ass, but that is partly due to his patronizing "the three-and-six-one-price hat company", and wearing a reach-me-down frock-coat. As for that perpetual brown velveteen jacket of Gowing's—why, he resembles an itinerant photographer.'

I said it was not the coat that made the gentleman; whereupon Lupin, with a laugh, replied: 'No, and it wasn't much of a gentleman who made their coats.'

We were rather jolly at supper, and Daisy made herself very agreeable, especially in the earlier part of the evening, when she sang. At supper, however, she said: 'Can you make tee-to-tums* with bread?' and she commenced rolling up pieces of bread, and twisting them round on the table. I felt this to be bad manners, but of course said nothing. Presently Daisy and Lupin, to my disgust, began throwing bread-pills at each other. Frank followed suit, and so did Cummings and Gowing, to my astonishment. They then commenced throwing hard pieces of crust, one piece catching me on the forehead, and making me blink. I said: 'Steady, please; steady!' Frank jumped up and said: 'Tum, tum; then the band played.'

I did not know what this meant, but they all roared, and continued the bread-battle. Gowing suddenly seized all the parsley off the cold mutton, and threw it full in my face. I looked daggers at Gowing, who replied: 'I say, it's no good trying to look indignant, with your hair full of parsley.' I rose from the table, and insisted that a stop should be put to this foolery at once. Frank Mutlar shouted: 'Time, gentlemen, please! time!' and turned out the gas, leaving us in absolute darkness.

I was feeling my way out of the room, when I suddenly received a hard intentional punch at the back of my head. I said loudly: 'Who did that?' There was no answer; so I repeated the question, with the same result. I struck a match, and lighted the gas. They were all talking and laughing, so I kept my own counsel; but, after they had gone, I said to Carrie: 'The person who sent me that insulting postcard at Christmas was here tonight.'

DECEMBER 29.—I had a most vivid dream last night. I woke up, and on falling asleep, dreamed the same dream over again precisely. I dreamt I heard Frank Mutlar telling his sister that he had not only sent me the insulting Christmas card, but admitted that he was the one who punched my head last night in the dark. As fate would have it, Lupin, at breakfast, was reading extracts from a letter he had just received from Frank.

I asked him to pass the envelope, that I might compare the writing. He did so, and I examined it by the side of the envelope containing the Christmas card. I detected a similarity in the writing, in spite of the attempted disguise. I passed them on to Carrie, who began to laugh. I asked her what she was laughing at, and she said the card was never directed to me at all. It was 'L. Pooter', not 'C. Pooter'. Lupin asked to look at the direction and the card, and exclaimed, with a laugh: 'Oh yes, Guv., it's meant for me.' I said: 'Are you in the habit of receiving insulting Christmas cards?' He replied: 'Oh yes, and of *sending* them, too.'

In the evening Gowing called, and said he enjoyed himself very much last night. I took the opportunity to confide in him, as an old friend, about the vicious punch last night. He burst out laughing, and said: 'Oh, it was *your head*, was it? I know I accidentally hit something; but I thought it was a brick wall.' I told him I felt hurt, in both senses of the expression.

DECEMBER 30, SUNDAY.—Lupin spent the whole day with the Mutlars. He seemed rather cheerful in the evening, so I said: 'I'm glad to see you so happy, Lupin.' He answered: 'Well, Daisy is a splendid girl, but I was obliged to take her old fool of a father down a peg. What with his meanness over his cigars, his stinginess over his drinks, his farthing economy in turning down the gas if you only quit the room for a second, writing to one on half-sheets of notepaper, sticking the remnant of the last cake of soap on to the new cake, putting two bricks on each side of the fireplace, and his general "outside-halfpenny-'bus-ness",* I was compelled to let him have a bit of my mind.' I said: 'Lupin, you are not much more than a boy; I hope you won't repent it.'

DECEMBER 31.—The last day of the Old Year. I received an extraordinary letter from Mr Mutlar, senior. He writes:

Dear Sir,
For a long time past I have had considerable difficulty deciding the important question, 'Who is the master of my own house? Myself, or *your son* Lupin?' Believe me, I have no prejudice one way or the other; but I have been most reluctantly compelled to give judgement to the effect that *I* am the master of it. Under the circumstances, it has become my duty to forbid your son to enter my house again. I am sorry, because it deprives me of the society of one of the most modest, unassuming, and gentlemanly persons I have ever had the honour of being acquainted with.

I did not desire the last day to wind up disagreeably, so I said nothing to either Carrie or Lupin about the letter.

A most terrible fog came on, and Lupin would go out in it, but promised to be back to drink out the Old Year—a custom we have always observed. At a quarter to twelve Lupin had not returned, and the fog was fearful. As time was drawing close, I got out the spirits. Carrie and I deciding on whisky, I opened a fresh bottle; but Carrie said it smelt like brandy. As I knew it to be whisky, I said there was nothing to discuss. Carrie, evidently vexed that Lupin had not come in, *did* discuss it all the same, and wanted me to have a small wager with her to decide by the smell. I said I could decide it by the taste in a moment. A silly and unnecessary argument followed, the result of which was we suddenly saw it was a quarter-past twelve, and, for the first time in our married life, we missed welcoming in the New Year. Lupin got home at a quarter-past two, having got lost in the fog—so he said.

CHAPTER XIV

Begin the year with an unexpected promotion at the office. I make two good jokes. I get an enormous rise in my salary. Lupin speculates successfully and starts a pony-trap. Have to speak to Sarah. Extraordinary conduct of Gowing's.

JANUARY 1.—I had intended concluding my diary last week; but a most important event has happened, so I shall continue for a little while longer on the flyleaves attached to the end of my last year's diary. It had just struck half-past one, and I was on the point of leaving the office to have my dinner, when I received a message that Mr Perkupp desired to see me at once. I must confess that my heart commenced to beat and I had most serious misgivings.

Mr Perkupp was in his room writing, and he said: 'Take a seat, Mr Pooter, I shall not be a moment.'

I replied: 'No, thank you, sir; I'll stand.' I watched the clock on the mantelpiece, and I was waiting quite twenty minutes; but it seemed hours. Mr Perkupp at last got up himself.

I said: 'I hope there is nothing wrong, sir?'

He replied: 'Oh dear, no! quite the reverse, I hope.' What a weight off my mind! My breath seemed to come back again in an instant.

Mr Perkupp said: 'Mr Buckling is going to retire, and there will be some slight changes in the office. You have been with us nearly twenty-one years, and, in consequence of your conduct during that period, we intend making a special promotion in your favour. We have not quite decided how you will be placed; but in any case there will be a considerable increase in your salary, which, it is quite unnecessary for me to say, you fully deserve. I have an appointment at two; but you shall hear more tomorrow.'

He then left the room quickly, and I was not even allowed time or thought to express a single word of grateful thanks to him. I need not say how dear Carrie received this joyful news. With perfect simplicity she said: 'At last we shall be able to have a chimney-glass for the back drawing-room, which we always wanted.' I added: 'Yes, and at last you shall have that little costume which you saw at Peter Robinson's* so cheap.'

JANUARY 2.—I was in a great state of suspense all day at the office. I did not like to worry Mr Perkupp; but as he did not send for me, and mentioned yesterday that he would see me again today, I thought it better, perhaps, to go to him. I knocked at his door, and on entering, Mr Perkupp said: 'Oh! it's you, Mr Pooter; do you want to see me?' I said: 'No, sir, I thought you wanted to see me!' 'Oh!' he replied, 'I remember. Well, I am very busy today; I will see you tomorrow.'

JANUARY 3.—Still in a state of anxiety and excitement, which was not alleviated by ascertaining that Mr Perkupp sent word he should not be at the office today. In the evening, Lupin, who was busily engaged with a paper, said suddenly to me: 'Do you know anything about *chalk pits*, Guv.?' I said: 'No, my boy, not that I'm aware of.' Lupin said: 'Well, I give you the tip; *chalk pits* are as safe as Consols,* and pay six per cent. at par.' I said a rather neat thing, viz.: 'They may be six per cent. at *par*, but your *pa* has no money to invest.' Carrie and I both roared with laughter. Lupin did not take the slightest notice of the joke, although I purposely repeated it for him; but continued: 'I give you the tip, that's all—*chalk pits*!' I said another funny thing: 'Mind you don't fall into them!' Lupin put on a supercilious smile, and said: 'Bravo! Joe Miller.'*

JANUARY 4.—Mr Perkupp sent for me and told me that my position would be that of one of the senior clerks. I was more than overjoyed. Mr Perkupp added, he would let me know tomorrow what the salary would be. This means another day's anxiety; I don't mind, for it is anxiety of the right sort. That reminded me that I had forgotten to speak to Lupin about the letter I received from Mr Mutlar, senr. I broached the subject to Lupin in the evening, having first consulted Carrie. Lupin was riveted to the *Financial News*,* as if he had been a born capitalist, and I said: 'Pardon me a moment, Lupin, how is it you have not been to the Mutlars' any day this week?'

Lupin answered: 'I told you! I cannot stand old Mutlar.'

I said: 'Mr Mutlar writes to me to say pretty plainly that he cannot stand you!'

Lupin said: 'Well, I like his cheek in writing to *you*. I'll find out if his father is still alive, and I will write *him* a note complaining of *his* son, and I'll state pretty clearly that his son is a blithering idiot!'

I said: 'Lupin, please moderate your expressions in the presence of your mother.'

Lupin said: 'I'm very sorry, but there is no other expression one can apply to him. However, I'm determined not to enter his place again.'

I said: 'You know, Lupin, he has forbidden you the house.'

Lupin replied: 'Well, we won't split straws—it's all the same. Daisy is a trump, and will wait for me ten years, if necessary.'

JANUARY 5.—I can scarcely write the news. Mr Perkupp told me my salary would be raised £100! I stood gaping for a moment unable to realize it. I annually get £10 rise, and I thought it might be £15 or even £20; but £100 surpasses all belief. Carrie and I both rejoiced over our good fortune. Lupin came home in the evening in the utmost good spirits. I sent Sarah quietly round to the grocer's for a bottle of champagne, the same as we had before, 'Jackson Frères.' It was opened at supper, and I said to Lupin: 'This is to celebrate some good news I have received today.' Lupin replied: 'Hooray, Guv.! And I have some good news, also; a double event, eh?' I said: 'My boy, as a result of twenty-one years' industry and strict attention to the interests of my superiors in office, I have been rewarded with promotion and a rise in salary of £100.'

Lupin gave three cheers, and we rapped the table furiously, which brought in Sarah to see what the matter was. Lupin ordered us to 'fill up' again, and addressing us upstanding, said: 'Having been in the firm of Job Cleanands, stock and share-brokers, a few weeks, and *not* having paid particular attention to the interests of my superiors in office, my Guv'nor, as a reward to me, allotted me £5 worth of shares in a really good thing. The result is, today I have made £200.' I said: 'Lupin, you are joking.' 'No, Guv., it's the good old truth; Job Cleanands *put me on to Chlorates*.'*

JANUARY 21.—I am very much concerned at Lupin having started a pony-trap. I said: 'Lupin, are you justified in this outrageous extravagance?' Lupin replied: 'Well, one must get to the City somehow. I've only hired it, and can give it up any time I like.' I repeated my question: 'Are you justified in this extravagance?' He replied: 'Look here, Guv.; excuse me saying so, but you're a bit out of date. It does not pay nowadays, fiddling about over small things. I don't mean anything personal, Guv'nor. My boss says if I take his tip, and stick to big things, I can make big money!' I said I thought the very idea of speculation most horrifying. Lupin said: 'It is not speculation, it's a dead cert.' I advised him, at all events, not to continue the pony and cart; but he replied: 'I made £200 in one day; now suppose I only make £200 in a month, or put it at £100 a month, which is ridiculously low—why, that is £1,250 a year. What's a few pounds a week for a trap?'

I did not pursue the subject further, beyond saying that I should feel glad when the autumn came, and Lupin would be of age and responsible for his own debts. He answered: 'My dear Guv., I promise you faithfully that I will never speculate with what I have not got. I shall only go on Job Cleanands' tips, and as he is in the "know" it is pretty safe sailing.' I felt somewhat relieved. Gowing called in the evening and, to my surprise, informed me that, as he had made £10 by one of Lupin's tips, he intended asking us and the Cummings round next Saturday. Carrie and I said we should be delighted.

JANUARY 22.—I don't generally lose my temper with servants; but I had to speak to Sarah rather sharply about a careless habit she has recently contracted of shaking the tablecloth, after removing the breakfast things, in a manner which causes all the crumbs to fall on the carpet, eventually to be trodden in. Sarah answered very rudely: 'Oh, you are always complaining.' I replied: 'Indeed, I am not. I spoke to you last week about walking all over the drawing-room carpet with a piece of yellow soap on the heel of your boot.' She said: 'And you're always grumbling about your breakfast.' I said: 'No, I am not; but I feel perfectly justified in complaining that I never can get a hard-boiled egg. The moment I crack the shell it spurts all over the plate, and I have spoken to you at least fifty times about it.' She began to cry and make a scene; but fortunately my 'bus came by, so I had a good excuse for leaving her. Gowing left a message in the evening, that we were not to forget next Saturday. Carrie amusingly said: 'As he has never asked any friends before, we are not likely to forget it.'

JANUARY 23.—I asked Lupin to try and change the hard brushes, he recently made me a present of, for some softer ones, as my hairdresser tells me I ought not to brush my hair too much just now.

JANUARY 24.—The new chimney-glass came home for the back drawing-room. Carrie arranged some fans very prettily on the top and on each side. It is an immense improvement to the room.

JANUARY 25.—We had just finished our tea, when who should come in but Cummings, who has not been here for over three weeks. I noticed that he looked anything but well, so I said: 'Well, Cummings, how are you? You look a little blue.' He replied: 'Yes! and I feel blue too.' I said: 'Why, what's the matter?' He said: 'Oh, nothing, except that I have been on my back for a couple of weeks, that's all. At one time my doctor nearly gave me up, yet not a soul has come near me. No one has even taken the trouble to enquire whether I was alive or dead.'

I said: 'This is the first I have heard of it. I have passed your house several nights, and presumed you had company, as the rooms were so brilliantly lighted.'

Cummings replied: 'No! The only company I have had was my wife, the doctor, and the landlady—the last-named having turned out a perfect trump. I wonder you did not see it in the paper. I know it was mentioned in the *Bicycle News*.'

I thought to cheer him up, and said: 'Well, you are all right now?'

He replied: 'That's not the question. The question is whether an illness does not enable you to discover who are your *true* friends.'

I said such an observation was unworthy of him. To make matters worse, in came Gowing, who gave Cummings a violent slap on the back, and said: 'Hulloh! Have you seen a ghost? You look scared to death, like Irving in *Macbeth*.'* I said: 'Gently, Gowing, the poor fellow has been very ill.' Gowing roared with laughter and said: 'Yes, and you look it, too.' Cummings quietly said: 'Yes, and I feel it too—not that I suppose you care.'

An awkward silence followed. Gowing said: 'Never mind, Cummings, you and the missis come round to my place tomorrow, and it will cheer you up a bit; for we'll open a bottle of wine.'

JANUARY 26.—An extraordinary thing happened. Carrie and I went round to Gowing's, as arranged, at half-past seven. We knocked and rang several times without getting an answer. At last the latch was drawn and the door opened a little way, the chain still being up. A man in shirt-sleeves put his head through and said: 'Who is it? What do you want?' I said: 'Mr Gowing, he is expecting us.' The man said (as well as I could hear, owing to the yapping of a little dog): 'I don't think he is. Mr Gowing is not at home.' I said: 'He will be in directly.'

With that observation he slammed the door, leaving Carrie and me standing on the steps with a cutting wind blowing round the corner.

Carrie advised me to knock again. I did so, and then discovered for the first time that the knocker had been newly painted, and the paint had come off on my gloves—which were, in consequence, completely spoiled.

I knocked at the door with my stick two or three times.

The man opened the door, taking the chain off this time, and began abusing me. He said: 'What do you mean by scratching the paint with your stick like that, spoiling the varnish? You ought to be ashamed of yourself.'

I said: 'Pardon me, Mr Gowing invited——'

He interrupted and said: 'I don't care for Mr Gowing, or any of his friends. This is *my* door, not Mr Gowing's. There are people here besides Mr Gowing.'

The impertinence of this man was nothing. I scarcely noticed it, it was so trivial in comparison with the scandalous conduct of Gowing.

At this moment Cummings and his wife arrived. Cummings was very lame and leaning on a stick; but got up the steps and asked what the matter was.

The man said: 'Mr Gowing said nothing about expecting anyone. All he said was he had just received an invitation to Croydon, and he should not be back till Monday evening. He took his bag with him.'

With that he slammed the door again. I was too indignant with Gowing's conduct to say anything. Cummings looked white with rage, and as he descended the steps struck his stick violently on the ground and said: 'Scoundrel!'

CHAPTER XV

Gowing explains his conduct. Lupin takes us for a drive, which we don't enjoy. Lupin introduces us to Mr Murray Posh.

FEBRUARY 8.—It does seem hard I cannot get good sausages for breakfast. They are either full of bread or spice, or are as red as beef. Still anxious about the £20 I invested last week by Lupin's advice. However, Cummings has done the same.

FEBRUARY 9.—Exactly a fortnight has passed, and I have neither seen nor heard from Gowing respecting his extraordinary conduct in asking us round to his house, and then being out. In the evening Carrie was engaged marking a half-dozen new collars* I had purchased. I'll back Carrie's marking against anybody's. While I was drying them at the fire, and Carrie was rebuking me for scorching them, Cummings came in.

He seemed quite well again, and chaffed us about marking the collars. I asked him if he had heard from Gowing, and he replied that he had not. I said I should not have believed that Gowing could have acted in such an ungentlemanly manner. Cummings said: 'You are mild in your description of him; I think he has acted like a cad.'

The words were scarcely out of his mouth when the door opened, and Gowing, putting in his head, said: 'May I come in?' I said: 'Certainly.' Carrie said very pointedly: 'Well, you *are* a stranger.' Gowing said: 'Yes, I've been on and off to Croydon during the last fortnight.' I could see Cummings was boiling over, and eventually he tackled Gowing very strongly respecting his conduct last Saturday week. Gowing appeared surprised, and said: 'Why, I posted a letter to you in the morning announcing that the party was "off, very much off".' I said: 'I never got it.' Gowing, turning to Carrie, said: 'I suppose letters sometimes *miscarry*, don't they, *Mrs Carrie*?' Cummings sharply said: 'This is not a time for joking. *I* had no notice of the party being put off.' Gowing replied: 'I told Pooter in my note to tell you, as I was in a hurry. However, I'll enquire at the post-office, and we must meet again at my place.' I added that I hoped he would be present at the next meeting. Carrie roared at this, and even Cummings could not help laughing.

FEBRUARY 10, SUNDAY.—Contrary to my wishes, Carrie allowed Lupin to persuade her to take her for a drive in the afternoon in his trap. I quite disapprove of driving on a Sunday, but I did not like to trust Carrie alone with Lupin, so I offered to go too. Lupin said: 'Now, that is nice of you, Guv., but you won't mind sitting on the back-seat of the cart?'

Lupin proceeded to put on a bright-blue coat that seemed miles too large for him. Carrie said it wanted taking in considerably at the back. Lupin said: 'Haven't you seen a box-coat* before? You can't drive in anything else.'

He may wear what he likes in the future, for I shall never drive with him again. His conduct was shocking. When we passed Highgate Archway, he tried to pass everything and everybody. He shouted to respectable people who were walking quietly in the road to get out of the way; he flicked at the horse of an old man who was riding, causing it to rear; and, as I had to ride backwards, I was compelled to face a gang of roughs in a donkey-cart, whom Lupin had chaffed, and who turned and followed us for nearly a mile, bellowing, indulging in coarse jokes and laughter, to say nothing of occasionally pelting us with orange-peel.

Lupin's excuse—that the Prince of Wales would have to put up with the same sort of thing if he drove to the Derby—was of little consolation to either Carrie or myself. Frank Mutlar called in the evening, and Lupin went out with him.

FEBRUARY 11.—Feeling a little concerned about Lupin, I mustered up courage to speak to Mr Perkupp about him. Mr Perkupp has always been most kind to me, so I told him everything, including yesterday's adventure. Mr Perkupp kindly replied: 'There is no necessity for you to be anxious, Mr Pooter. It would be impossible for a son of such good parents to turn out erroneously. Remember he is young, and will soon get older. I wish we could find room for him in this firm.' The advice of this good man takes loads off my mind. In the evening Lupin came in.

After our little supper, he said: 'My dear parents, I have some news, which I fear will affect you considerably.' I felt a qualm come over me, and said nothing. Lupin then said: 'It may distress you—in fact, I'm sure it will—but this afternoon I have given up my pony and trap for ever.' It may seem absurd but I was so pleased, I immediately opened a bottle of port. Gowing dropped in just in time, bringing with him a large sheet, with a print of a tailless donkey, which he fastened against the wall. He then produced several separate tails, and we spent the remainder of the evening trying blindfolded to pin a tail on in the proper place. My sides positively ached with laughter when I went to bed.

FEBRUARY 12.—In the evening I spoke to Lupin about his engagement with Daisy Mutlar. I asked if he had heard from her. He replied: 'No; she promised that old windbag of a father of hers that she would not communicate with me. I see Frank Mutlar, of course; in fact, he said he might call again this evening.' Frank called, but said he could not stop, as he had a friend waiting outside for him, named

Mr Murray Posh

Murray Posh, adding he was quite a swell. Carrie asked Frank to bring him in.

He was brought in, Gowing entering at the same time. Mr Murray Posh was a tall, fat young man, and was evidently of a very nervous disposition, as he subsequently confessed he would never go in a hansom cab,* nor would he enter a four-wheeler until the driver had first got on the box with his reins in his hands.

On being introduced, Gowing, with his usual want of tact, said: 'Any relation to "Posh's three-shilling hats"?' Mr Posh replied: 'Yes; but please understand I don't try on hats myself. I take no *active* part in the business.' I replied: 'I wish I had a business like it.' Mr Posh seemed pleased, and gave a long but most interesting history of the extraordinary difficulties in the manufacture of cheap hats.

Murray Posh evidently knew Daisy Mutlar very intimately from the way he was talking of her; and Frank said to Lupin once, laughingly: 'If you don't look out, Posh will cut you out!' When they had all gone, I referred to this flippant conversation; and Lupin said, sarcastically: 'A man who is jealous has no respect for himself. A man who would be jealous of an elephant like Murray Posh could only have a contempt for himself. I know Daisy. She *would* wait ten years for me, as I said before; in fact, if necessary, *she would wait twenty years for me.*'

CHAPTER XVI

We lose money over Lupin's advice as to investment, so does Cummings. Murray Posh engaged to Daisy Mutlar.

FEBRUARY 18.—Carrie has several times recently called attention to the thinness of my hair at the top of my head, and recommended me to get it seen to. I was this morning trying to look at it by the aid of a small hand-glass, when somehow my elbow caught against the edge of the chest of drawers and knocked the glass out of my hand and smashed it. Carrie was in an awful way about it, as she is rather absurdly superstitious. To make matters worse, my large photograph in the drawing-room fell during the night, and the glass cracked.

Carrie said: 'Mark my words, Charles, some misfortune is about to happen.'

I said: 'Nonsense, dear.'

In the evening Lupin arrived home early, and seemed a little agitated. I said: 'What's up, my boy?' He hesitated a good deal, and then said: 'You know those Parachikka Chlorates I advised you to invest £20 in?' I replied: 'Yes, they are all right, I trust?' He replied: 'Well, no! To the surprise of everybody, they have utterly collapsed.'

My breath was so completely taken away, I could say nothing. Carrie looked at me, and said: 'What did I tell you?' Lupin, after a while, said: 'However, you are specially fortunate. I received an early tip, and sold out yours immediately, and was fortunate to get £2 for them. So you get something after all.'

I gave a sigh of relief. I said: 'I was not so sanguine as to suppose, as you predicted, that I should get six or eight times the amount of my investment; still a profit of £2 is a good percentage for such a short time.' Lupin said, quite irritably: 'You don't understand. I sold your £20 shares for £2; you therefore lose £18 on the transaction, whereby Cummings and Gowing will lose the whole of theirs.'

FEBRUARY 19.—Lupin, before going to town, said: 'I am very sorry about those Parachikka Chlorates; it would not have happened if the boss, Job Cleanands, had been in town. Between ourselves, you must not be surprised if something goes wrong at our office. Job Cleanands has not been seen the last few days, and it strikes me several people *do* want to see him very particularly.'

In the evening Lupin was just on the point of going out to avoid a collision with Gowing and Cummings, when the former entered the room, without knocking, but with his usual trick of saying, 'May I come in?'

He entered, and to the surprise of Lupin and myself, seemed to be in the very best of spirits. Neither Lupin nor I broached the subject to him, but he did so of his own accord. He said: 'I say, those Parachikka Chlorates have gone an awful smash! You're a nice one, Master Lupin. How much do you lose?' Lupin, to my utter astonishment, said: 'Oh! I had nothing in them. There was some informality in my application—I forgot to enclose the cheque or something, and I didn't get any. The Guv. loses £18.' I said: 'I quite understood you were in it, or nothing would have induced me to speculate.' Lupin replied: 'Well, it can't be helped; you must go double on the next tip.' Before I could reply, Gowing said: 'Well, I lose nothing, fortunately. From what I heard, I did not quite believe in them, so I persuaded Cummings to take my £15 worth, as he had more faith in them than I had.'

Lupin burst out laughing, and, in the most unseemly manner, said: 'Alas, poor Cummings! He'll lose £35.' At that moment there was a ring at the bell. Lupin said: 'I don't want to meet Cummings.' If he had gone out of the door he would have met him in the passage, so as quickly as possible Lupin opened the parlour window and got out. Gowing jumped up suddenly, exclaiming: 'I don't want to see him either!' and, before I could say a word, he followed Lupin out of the window.

For my own part, I was horrified to think my own son and one of my most intimate friends should depart from the house like a couple of interrupted burglars. Poor Cummings was very upset, and of course was naturally very angry both with Lupin and Gowing. I pressed him to have a little whisky, and he replied that he had given up whisky; but would like a little 'Unsweetened', as he was advised it was the most healthy spirit. I had none in the house, but sent Sarah round to Lockwood's for some.

FEBRUARY 20.—The first thing that caught my eye on opening the *Standard* was—'Great Failure of Stock and Share Dealers! Mr Job

Cleanands Absconded!' I handed it to Carrie and she replied: 'Oh! perhaps it's for Lupin's good. I never did think it a suitable situation for him.' I thought the whole affair very shocking.

Lupin came down to breakfast, and seeing he looked painfully distressed, I said: 'We know the news, my dear boy, and feel very sorry for you.' Lupin said: 'How did you know? who told you?' I handed him the *Standard*. He threw the paper down, and said: 'Oh I don't care a button for that! I expected that, but I did not expect this.' He then read a letter from Frank Mutlar, announcing, in a cool manner, that Daisy Mutlar is to be married next month to Murray Posh. I exclaimed, 'Murray Posh! Is not that the very man Frank had the impudence to bring here last Tuesday week?' Lupin said: 'Yes; the *"Posh's-three-shilling-hats"* chap.'

We all then ate our breakfast in dead silence.

In fact, I could eat nothing. I was not only too worried, but I cannot and will not eat cushion of bacon.* If I cannot get streaky bacon, I will do without anything.

When Lupin rose to go I noticed a malicious smile creep over his face. I asked him what it meant. He replied: 'Oh! only a little consolation—still it *is* a consolation. I have just remembered that, by *my* advice, Mr Murray Posh has invested £600 in Parachikka Chlorates!'

CHAPTER XVII

Marriage of Daisy Mutlar and Murray Posh. The dream of my life realised. Mr Perkupp takes Lupin into the office.

MARCH 20.—Today being the day on which Daisy Mutlar and Mr Murray Posh are to be married, Lupin has gone with a friend to spend the day at Gravesend. Lupin has been much cut-up over the affair, although he declares that he is glad it is off. I wish he would not go to so many music-halls, but one dare not say anything to him about it. At the present moment he irritates me by singing all over the house some nonsense about 'What's the matter with Gladstone? He's all right! What's the matter with Lupin? He's all right!' *I* don't think either of them is. In the evening Gowing called, and the chief topic of conversation was Daisy's marriage to Murray Posh. I said: 'I was glad the matter was at an end, as Daisy would only have made a fool of Lupin.' Gowing, with his usual good taste, said: 'Oh, Master Lupin can make a fool of himself without any assistance.' Carrie very properly resented this, and Gowing had sufficient sense to say he was sorry.

MARCH 21.—Today I shall conclude my diary, for it is one of the happiest days of my life. My great dream of the last few weeks—in fact, of many years—has been realized. This morning came a letter from Mr Perkupp, asking me to take Lupin down to the office with me. I went to Lupin's room; poor fellow, he seemed very pale, and said he had a bad headache. He had come back yesterday from Gravesend, where he spent part of the day in a small boat on the water, having been mad enough to neglect to take his overcoat with him. I showed him Mr Perkupp's letter, and he got up as quickly as possible. I begged of him not to put on his fast-coloured clothes and ties, but to dress in something black or quiet-looking.

Carrie was all of a tremble when she read the letter, and all she could keep on saying was: 'Oh, I *do* hope it will be all right.' For myself, I could scarcely eat any breakfast. Lupin came down dressed quietly, and looking a perfect gentleman, except that his face was rather yellow. Carrie, by way of encouragement said: 'You do look nice, Lupin.' Lupin replied: 'Yes, it's a good make-up, isn't it? A regular-downright-respectable-funereal-first-class-City-firm-junior-clerk.' He laughed rather ironically.

In the hall I heard a great noise, and also Lupin shouting to Sarah to fetch down his old hat. I went into the passage, and found Lupin in a fury, kicking and smashing a new tall hat. I said: 'Lupin, my boy, what are you doing? How wicked of you! Some poor fellow would be glad to have it.' Lupin replied: 'I would not insult any poor fellow by giving it to him.'

When he had gone outside, I picked up the battered hat, and saw inside 'Posh's Patent'. Poor Lupin! I can forgive him. It seemed hours before we reached the office. Mr Perkupp sent for Lupin, who was with him nearly an hour. He returned, as I thought, crestfallen in appearance. I said: 'Well, Lupin, how about Mr Perkupp?' Lupin commenced his song: 'What's the matter with Perkupp? He's all right!' I felt instinctively my boy was engaged. I went to Mr Perkupp, but I could not speak. He said: 'Well, Mr Pooter, what is it?' I must have looked a fool, for all I could say was: 'Mr Perkupp, you are a good man.' He looked at me for a moment, and said: 'No, Mr Pooter, *you* are the good man; and we'll see if we cannot get your son to follow such an excellent example.' I said: 'Mr Perkupp, may I go home? I cannot work any more today.'

My good master shook my hand warmly as he nodded his head. It was as much as I could do to prevent myself from crying in the 'bus; in fact, I should have done so, had my thoughts not been interrupted by Lupin, who was having a quarrel with a fat man in the 'bus, whom he accused of taking up too much room.

In the evening Carrie sent round for dear old friend Cummings and his wife, and also to Gowing. We all sat round the fire, and in a bottle of 'Jackson Frères', which Sarah fetched from the grocer's, drank Lupin's health. I lay awake for hours, thinking of the future. My boy in the same office as myself—we can go down together by the 'bus, come home together, and who knows but in the course of time he may take great interest in our little home. That he may help me to put a nail in here or a nail in there, or help his dear mother to hang a picture. In the summer he may help us in our little garden with the flowers, and assist us to paint the stands and pots.

(By-the-by, I must get in some more enamel paint.) All this I thought over and over again, and a thousand happy thoughts beside. I heard the clock strike four, and soon after fell asleep, only to dream of three happy people—Lupin, dear Carrie, and myself.

CHAPTER XVIII

Trouble with a stylographic pen. We go to a Volunteer Ball, where I am let in for an expensive supper. Grossly insulted by a cabman. An odd invitation to Southend.

APRIL 8.—No events of any importance, except that Gowing strongly recommended a new patent stylographic pen,* which cost me nine-and-sixpence, and which was simply nine-and-sixpence thrown in the mud. It has caused me constant annoyance and irritability of temper. The ink oozes out of the top, making a mess on my hands, and once at the office when I was knocking the palm of my hand on the desk to jerk the ink down, Mr Perkupp, who had just entered, called out: 'Stop that knocking! I suppose that is you, Mr Pitt?' That young monkey, Pitt, took a malicious glee in responding quite loudly: 'No, sir; I beg pardon, it is Mr Pooter with his pen; it has been going on all the morning.' To make matters worse, I saw Lupin laughing behind his desk. I thought it wiser to say nothing. I took the pen back to the shop and asked them if they would take it back, as it did not act. I did not expect the full price returned, but was willing to take half. The man said he could not do that—buying and selling were two different things. Lupin's conduct during the period he has been in Mr Perkupp's office has been most exemplary. My only fear is, it is too good to last.

APRIL 9.—Gowing called, bringing with him an invitation for Carrie and myself to a ball given by the East Acton Rifle Brigade, which he thought would be a swell affair, as the member for East Acton (Sir William Grime) had promised his patronage. We accepted of his kindness, and he stayed to supper, an occasion I thought suitable for trying a bottle of the sparkling Algéra that Mr James (of Sutton) had sent as a present. Gowing sipped the wine, observing that he had never tasted it before, and further remarked that his policy was to stick to more recognized brands. I told him it was a present from a dear friend, and one mustn't look a gift-horse in the mouth.

Gowing facetiously replied: 'And he didn't like putting it in the mouth either.'

I thought the remarks were rude without being funny, but on tasting it myself, came to the conclusion there was some justification for them. The sparkling Algéra is very like cider, only more sour. I suggested that perhaps the thunder had turned it a bit acid. He merely replied: 'Oh! I don't think so.' We had a very pleasant game of cards, though I lost four shillings and Carrie lost one, and Gowing said he had lost about sixpence: how *he* could have lost, considering that Carrie and I were the only other players, remains a mystery.

APRIL 14, SUNDAY.—Owing, I presume, to the unsettled weather, I awoke with a feeling that my skin was drawn over my face as tight as a drum. Walking round the garden with Mr and Mrs Treane, members of our congregation who had walked back with us, I was much annoyed to find a large newspaper full of bones on the gravel-path, evidently thrown over by those young Griffin boys next door; who, whenever we have friends, climb up the empty steps inside their conservatory, tap at the windows, making faces, whistling, and imitating birds.

APRIL 15.—Burnt my tongue most awfully with the Worcester sauce,* through that stupid girl Sarah shaking the bottle violently before putting it on the table.

APRIL 16.—The night of the East Acton Volunteer Ball. On my advice, Carrie put on the same dress that she looked so beautiful in at the Mansion House, for it had occurred to me, being a military ball, that Mr Perkupp, who, I believe, is an officer in the Honorary Artillery Company, would in all probability be present. Lupin, in his usual incomprehensible language, remarked that he had heard it was a 'bounders' ball'.* I didn't ask him what he meant though I didn't understand. Where he gets these expressions from I don't know; he certainly doesn't learn them at home.

The invitation was for half-past eight, so I concluded if we arrived an hour later we should be in good time, without being 'unfashionable', as Mrs James says. It was very difficult to find—the cabman having to get down several times to enquire at different public-

Young Griffin boys making faces, whistling, and imitating birds

houses where the Drill Hall was. I wonder at people living in such
out-of-the-way places. No one seemed to know it. However, after
going up and down a good many badly-lighted streets we arrived at
our destination. I had no idea it was so far from Holloway. I gave the
cabman five shillings, who only grumbled, saying it was dirt cheap at
half-a-sovereign, and was impertinent enough to advise me the next
time I went to a ball to take a 'bus.

Captain Welcut received us, saying we were rather late, but that
it was better late than never. He seemed a very good-looking gentleman though, as Carrie remarked, 'rather short for an officer'.
He begged to be excused for leaving us, as he was engaged for
a dance, and hoped we should make ourselves at home. Carrie took
my arm and we walked round the rooms two or three times and
watched the people dancing. I couldn't find a single person I knew,
but attributed it to most of them being in uniform. As we were
entering the supper-room I received a slap on the shoulder, followed

by a welcome shake of the hand. I said: 'Mr Padge, I believe'; he replied, 'That's right.'

I gave Carrie a chair, and seated by her was a lady who made herself at home with Carrie at once.

There was a very liberal repast on the tables, plenty of champagne, claret, etc., and, in fact, everything seemed to be done regardless of expense. Mr Padge is a man that, I admit, I have no particular liking for, but I felt so glad to come across someone I knew, that I asked him to sit at our table, and I must say that for a short fat man he looked well in uniform, although I think his tunic was rather baggy in the back. It was the only supper-room that I have been in that was not overcrowded; in fact we were the only people there, everybody being so busy dancing.

I assisted Carrie and her newly-formed acquaintance, who said her name was Lupkin, to some champagne; also myself, and handed the bottle to Mr Padge to do likewise, saying: 'You must look after yourself.' He replied: 'That's right,' and poured out half a tumbler and drank Carrie's health, coupled, as he said, 'with her worthy lord and master'. We all had some splendid pigeon pie, and ices to follow.

The waiters were very attentive, and asked if we would like some more wine. I assisted Carrie and her friend and Mr Padge, also some people who had just come from the dancing-room, who were very civil. It occurred to me at the time that perhaps some of the gentlemen knew me in the City, as they were so polite. I made myself useful, and assisted several ladies to ices, remembering an old saying that 'There is nothing lost by civility.'

The band struck up for the dance, and they all went into the ballroom. The ladies (Carrie and Mrs Lupkin) were anxious to see the dancing, and as I had not quite finished my supper, Mr Padge offered his arms to them and escorted them to the ballroom, telling me to follow. I said to Mr Padge: 'It is quite a West End affair,' to which remark Mr Padge replied: 'That's right.'

When I had quite finished my supper, and was leaving, the waiter who had been attending on us arrested my attention by tapping me on the shoulder. I thought it unusual for a waiter at a private ball to expect a tip, but nevertheless gave a shilling, as he had been very attentive. He smilingly replied: 'I beg your pardon, sir, this is no good,' alluding to the shilling. 'Your party's had four suppers at 5s. a head, five ices at 1s., three bottles of champagne at 11s. 6d., a glass of claret, and a sixpenny cigar for the stout gentleman—in all £3 0s. 6d.!'

I don't think I was ever so surprised in my life, and had only sufficient breath to inform him that I had received a private invitation, to which he answered that he was perfectly well aware of that; but that the invitation didn't include eatables and drinkables. A gentleman who was standing at the bar corroborated the waiter's statement, and assured me it was quite correct.

The waiter said he was extremely sorry if I had been under any misapprehension; but it was not his fault. Of course there was nothing to be done but to pay. So, after turning out my pockets, I just managed to scrape up sufficient, all but nine shillings; but the manager, on my giving my card to him, said: 'That's all right.'

I don't think I ever felt more humiliated in my life, and I determined to keep this misfortune from Carrie, for it would entirely destroy the pleasant evening she was enjoying. I felt there was no more enjoyment for me that evening, and it being late, I sought Carrie and Mrs Lupkin. Carrie said she was quite ready to go, and Mrs Lupkin, as we were wishing her 'Good-night,' asked Carrie and myself if we ever paid a visit to Southend? On my replying that I hadn't been there for many years, she very kindly said: 'Well, why don't you come down and stay at our place?' As her invitation was so pressing, and observing that Carrie wished to go, we promised we would visit her the next Saturday week, and stay till Monday. Mrs Lupkin said she would write to us tomorrow, giving us the address and particulars of trains, etc.

When we got outside the Drill Hall it was raining so hard that the roads resembled canals, and I need hardly say we had great difficulty in getting a cabman to take us to Holloway. After waiting a bit, a man said he would drive us, anyhow, as far as 'The Angel', at Islington, and we could easily get another cab from there. It was a tedious journey; the rain was beating against the windows and trickling down the inside of the cab.

When we arrived at 'The Angel' the horse seemed tired out. Carrie got out and ran into a doorway, and when I came to pay, to my absolute horror I remembered I had no money, nor had Carrie. I explained to the cabman how we were situated. Never in my life have I ever been so insulted; the cabman, who was a rough bully and to my thinking not sober, called me every name he could lay his tongue to, and positively seized me by the beard, which he pulled till the tears came into my eyes. I took the number of a policeman (who witnessed the assault) for not taking the man in charge. The policeman said he couldn't interfere, that he had seen no assault, and that people should not ride in cabs without money.

We had to walk home in the pouring rain, nearly two miles, and when I got in I put down the conversation I had with the cabman, word for word, as I intend writing to the *Telegraph* for the purpose of proposing that cabs should be driven only by men under Government control, to prevent civilians being subjected to the disgraceful insult and outrage that I had had to endure.

APRIL 17.—No water in our cistern again. Sent for Putley, who said he would soon remedy that, the cistern being zinc.

APRIL 18.—Water all right again in the cistern. Mrs James, of Sutton, called in the afternoon. She and Carrie draped the mantel-piece in the drawing-room, and put little toy spiders, frogs and bee-tles all over it, as Mrs James says it's quite the fashion. It was Mrs James' suggestion, and of course Carrie always does what Mrs James suggests. For my part, I preferred the mantelpiece as it was; but there, I'm a plain man, and don't pretend to be in the fashion.

APRIL 19.—Our next-door neighbour, Mr Griffin, called, and in a rather offensive tone accused me, or 'someone', of boring a hole in his cistern and letting out his water to supply our cistern, which adjoined his. He said he should have his repaired, and send us in the bill.

APRIL 20.—Cummings called, hobbling in with a stick, saying he had been on his back for a week. It appears he was trying to shut his bedroom door, which is situated just at the top of the staircase, and unknown to him a piece of cork the dog had been playing with had got between the door, and prevented it shutting; and in pulling the door hard, to give it an extra slam, the handle came off in his hands, and he fell backwards downstairs.

On hearing this, Lupin suddenly jumped up from the couch and rushed out of the room sideways. Cummings looked very indignant, and remarked it was very poor fun a man nearly breaking his back; and though I had my suspicions that Lupin was laughing, I assured

Cummings that he had only run out to open the door to a friend he expected. Cummings said this was the second time he had been laid up, and we had never sent to enquire. I said I knew nothing about it. Cummings said: 'It was mentioned in the *Bicycle News*.'

APRIL 22.—I have of late frequently noticed Carrie rubbing her nails a good deal with an instrument, and on asking her what she was doing, she replied: 'Oh, I'm going in for manicuring. It's all the fashion now.' I said: 'I suppose Mrs James introduced that into your head.' Carrie laughingly replied: 'Yes; but everyone does it now.'

I wish Mrs James wouldn't come to the house. Whenever she does she always introduces some new-fandangled rubbish into Carrie's head. One of these days I feel sure I shall tell her she's not welcome. I am sure it was Mrs James who put Carrie up to writing on dark slate-coloured paper with white ink. Nonsense!

APRIL 23.—Received a letter from Mrs Lupkin, of Southend, telling us the train to come by on Saturday, and hoping we will keep our promise to stay with her. The letter concluded: 'You must come and stay at our house; we shall charge you half what you will have to pay at the Royal, and the view is every bit as good.' Looking at the address at the top of the notepaper, I found it was: 'Lupkin's Family and Commercial Hotel.'

I wrote a note, saying we were compelled to 'decline her kind invitation'. Carrie thought this very satirical, and to the point.

By-the-by, I will never choose another cloth pattern at night. I ordered a new suit of dittos for the garden at Edwards', and chose the pattern by gaslight, and they seemed to be a quiet pepper-and-salt mixture with white stripes down. They came home this morning, and, to my horror, I found it was quite a flash-looking suit. There was a lot of green with bright yellow-coloured stripes.

I tried on the coat, and was annoyed to find Carrie giggling. She said: 'What mixture did you say you asked for?'

I said: 'A quiet pepper and salt.'

Carrie said: 'Well, it looks more like mustard, if you want to know the truth.'

CHAPTER XIX

Meet Teddy Finsworth, an old schoolfellow. We have a pleasant and quiet dinner at his uncle's, marred only by a few awkward mistakes on my part respecting Mr Finsworth's pictures. A discussion on dreams.

APRIL 27.—Kept a little later than usual at the office, and as I was hurrying along a man stopped me, saying: 'Hulloh! That's a face I know.' I replied politely: 'Very likely; lots of people know *me*, although I may not know them.' He replied: 'But you know *me*— Teddy Finsworth.' So it was. He was at the same school with me. I had not seen him for years and years. No wonder I did not know him! At school he was at least a head taller than I was; now I am at least a head taller than he is, and he has a thick beard, almost grey. He insisted on my having a glass of wine (a thing I never do), and told me he lived at Middlesboro', where he was Deputy Town Clerk, a position which was as high as the Town Clerk of London—in fact, higher. He added that he was staying for a few days in London, with his uncle, Mr Edgar Paul Finsworth (of Finsworth and Pultwell). He said he was sure his uncle would be only too pleased to see me, and he had a nice house, Watney Lodge, only a few minutes' walk from Muswell Hill Station. I gave him our address, and we parted.

In the evening, to my surprise, he called with a very nice letter from Mr Finsworth, saying if we (including Carrie) would dine with them tomorrow (Sunday), at two o'clock, he would be delighted. Carrie did not like to go; but Teddy Finsworth pressed us so much we consented. Carrie sent Sarah round to the butcher's and countermanded our half-leg of mutton, which we had ordered for tomorrow.

APRIL 28, SUNDAY.—We found Watney Lodge further off than we anticipated, and only arrived as the clock struck two, both feeling hot and uncomfortable. To make matters worse, a large collie dog pounced forward to receive us. He barked loudly and jumped up at Carrie, covering her light skirt, which she was wearing for the first time, with mud. Teddy Finsworth came out and drove the dog off and apologized. We were shown into the drawing-room, which was

beautifully decorated. It was full of knick-knacks, and some plates
hung up on the wall. There were several little wooden milk-stools
with paintings on them; also a white wooden banjo, painted by one of
Mr Paul Finsworth's nieces—a cousin of Teddy's.

Mr Paul Finsworth seemed quite a distinguished-looking elderly
gentleman, and was most gallant to Carrie. There were a great many
water-colours hanging on the walls, mostly different views of India,
which were very bright. Mr Finsworth said they were painted by
'Simpz',* and added that he was no judge of pictures himself but had
been informed on good authority that they were worth some hun-
dreds of pounds, although he had only paid a few shillings apiece for
them, frames included, at a sale in the neighbourhood.

There was also a large picture in a very handsome frame, done in
coloured crayons. It looked like a religious subject. I was very much
struck with the lace collar, it looked so real, but I unfortunately made
the remark that there was something about the expression of the face
that was not quite pleasing. It looked pinched. Mr Finsworth sorrow-
fully replied: 'Yes, the face was done after death—my wife's sister.'

I felt terribly awkward and bowed apologetically, and in a whisper
said I hoped I had not hurt his feelings. We both stood looking at the
picture for a few minutes in silence, when Mr Finsworth took out a
handkerchief and said: 'She was sitting in our garden last summer,'
and blew his nose violently. He seemed quite affected, so I turned to
look at something else and stood in front of a portrait of a jolly-looking
middle-aged gentleman, with a red face and straw hat. I said to Mr
Finsworth: 'Who is this jovial-looking gentleman? Life doesn't seem
to trouble him much.' Mr Finsworth said: 'No, it doesn't. *He is dead
too*—my brother.'

I was absolutely horrified at my own awkwardness. Fortunately at
this moment Carrie entered with Mrs Finsworth, who had taken her
upstairs to take off her bonnet and brush her skirt. Teddy said: 'Short
is late,' but at that moment the gentleman referred to arrived, and I
was introduced to him by Teddy, who said: 'Do you know Mr Short?'
I replied, smiling, that I had not that pleasure, but I hoped it would
not be *long* before I knew Mr *Short*. He evidently did not see my little
joke, although I repeated it twice with a little laugh. I suddenly
remembered it was Sunday, and Mr Short was perhaps *very particular*.

In this I was mistaken, for he was not at all particular in several of
his remarks after dinner. In fact I was so ashamed of one of his
observations that I took the opportunity to say to Mrs Finsworth that

'He is dead too.'

I feared she found Mr Short occasionally a little embarrassing. To my surprise she said: 'Oh! he is privileged you know.' I did *not* know as a matter of fact, and so I bowed apologetically. I fail to see why Mr Short should be privileged.

Another thing that annoyed me at dinner was that the collie dog, which jumped up at Carrie, was allowed to remain under the dining-room table. It kept growling and snapping at my boots every time I moved my foot. Feeling nervous rather, I spoke to Mrs Finsworth about the animal, and she remarked: 'It is only his play.' She jumped up and let in a frightfully ugly-looking spaniel called Bibbs, which had been scratching at the door. This dog also seemed to take a fancy to my boots, and I discovered afterwards that it had licked off every bit of blacking from them. I was positively ashamed of being seen in them. Mrs Finsworth, who, I must say, is not much of a Job's comforter,* said: 'Oh! we are used to Bibbs doing that to our visitors.'

Mr Finsworth had up some fine port, although I question whether it is a good thing to take on the top of beer. It made me feel a little sleepy, while it had the effect of inducing Mr Short to become 'privileged' to rather an alarming extent. It being cold even for April, there was a fire in the drawing-room; we sat round in easy-chairs, and Teddy and I waxed rather eloquent over the old school-days, which had the effect of sending all the others to sleep. I was delighted, as far as Mr Short was concerned, that it *did* have that effect on him.

We stayed till four, and the walk home was remarkable only for the fact that several fools giggled at the unpolished state of my boots. Polished them myself when I got home. Went to church in the evening, and could scarcely keep awake. I will not take port on top of beer again.

APRIL 29.—I am getting quite accustomed to being snubbed by Lupin, and I do not mind being sat upon by Carrie, because I think she has a certain amount of right to do so; but I do think it hard to be at once snubbed by wife, son, and both my guests.

Gowing and Cummings had dropped in during the evening, and I suddenly remembered an extraordinary dream I had a few nights ago, and I thought I would tell them about it. I dreamt I saw some huge blocks of ice in a shop with a bright glare behind them. I walked into the shop and the heat was overpowering. I found that the blocks of ice were on fire. The whole thing was so real and yet so supernatural I woke up in a cold perspiration. Lupin in a most contemptuous manner, said: 'What utter rot.'

Before I could reply, Gowing said there was nothing so completely uninteresting as other people's dreams.

I appealed to Cummings, but he said he was bound to agree with the others and my dream was especially nonsensical. I said: 'It seemed so real to me.' Gowing replied: 'Yes, to *you* perhaps, but not to *us*.' Whereupon they all roared.

Carrie, who had hitherto been quiet, said: 'He tells me his stupid dreams every morning nearly.' I replied: 'Very well, dear, I promise you I will never tell you or anybody else another dream of mine the longest day I live.' Lupin said: 'Hear! hear!' and helped himself to another glass of beer. The subject was fortunately changed, and Cummings read a most interesting article on the superiority of the bicycle to the horse.

CHAPTER XX

Dinner at Franching's to meet Mr Hardfur Huttle.

MAY 10.—Received a letter from Mr Franching, of Peckham,* asking us to dine with him tonight, at seven o'clock, to meet Mr Hardfur Huttle, a very clever writer for the American papers. Franching apologized for the short notice; but said he had at the last moment been disappointed of two of his guests and regarded us as old friends who would not mind filling up the gap. Carrie rather demurred at the invitation; but I explained to her that Franching was very well off and influential, and we could not afford to offend him. 'And we are sure to get a good dinner and a good glass of champagne.' 'Which never agrees with you!' Carrie replied, sharply. I regarded Carrie's observation as unsaid. Mr Franching asked us to wire a reply. As he had said nothing about dress in the letter, I wired back: 'With pleasure. Is it full dress?' and by leaving out our name, just got the message within the sixpence.

Got back early to give time to dress, which we received a telegram instructing us to do. I wanted Carrie to meet me at Franching's house; but she would not do so, so I had to go home to fetch her. What a long journey it is from Holloway to Peckham! Why do people live such a long way off? Having to change 'buses, I allowed plenty of time—in fact, too much; for we arrived at twenty minutes to seven, and Franching, so the servant said, had only just gone up to dress. However, he was down as the clock struck seven; he must have dressed very quickly.

I must say it was quite a distinguished party, and although we did not know anybody personally, they all seemed to be quite swells. Franching had got a professional waiter, and evidently spared no expense. There were flowers on the table round some fairy-lamps and the effect, I must say, was exquisite. The wine was good and there was plenty of champagne, concerning which Franching said he, himself, never wished to taste better. We were ten in number, and a menu card to each. One lady said she always preserved the menu and got the guests to write their names on the back.

We all of us followed her example, except Mr Huttle, who was of course the important guest.

The dinner-party consisted of Mr Franching, Mr Hardfur Huttle, Mr and Mrs Samuel Hillbutter, Mrs Field, Mr and Mrs Purdick, Mr Pratt, Mr R. Kent, and, last but not least, Mr and Mrs Charles Pooter. Franching said he was sorry he had no lady for me to take in to dinner. I replied that I preferred it, which I afterwards thought was a very uncomplimentary observation to make.

I sat next to Mrs Field at dinner. She seemed a well-informed lady, but was very deaf. It did not much matter, for Mr Hardfur Huttle did all the talking. He is a marvellously intellectual man and says things which from other people would seem quite alarming. How I wish I could remember even a quarter of his brilliant conversation. I made a few little reminding notes on the menu card.

One observation struck me as being absolutely powerful—though not to my way of thinking of course. Mrs Purdick happened to say:

"'Orthodox' is a grandiloquent word'

'You are certainly unorthodox, Mr Huttle.' Mr Huttle, with a peculiar expression (I can see it now) said in a slow rich voice: 'Mrs Purdick, "orthodox" is a grandiloquent word implying sticking-in-the-mud. If Columbus and Stephenson* had been orthodox, there would neither have been the discovery of America nor the steam-engine.' There was quite a silence. It appeared to me that such teaching was absolutely dangerous, and yet I felt—in fact we must all have felt—there was no answer to the argument. A little later on, Mrs Purdick, who is Franching's sister and also acted as hostess, rose from the table, and Mr Huttle said: 'Why, ladies, do you deprive us of your company so soon? Why not wait while we have our cigars?'

The effect was electrical. The ladies (including Carrie) were in no way inclined to be deprived of Mr Huttle's fascinating society, and immediately resumed their seats, amid much laughter and a little chaff. Mr Huttle said: 'Well, that's a real good sign; you shall not be insulted by being called orthodox any longer.' Mrs Purdick, who seemed to be a bright and rather sharp woman, said: 'Mr Huttle, we will meet you half-way—that is, till you get half-way through your cigar. That, at all events, will be the happy medium.'

I shall never forget the effect the words, 'happy medium', had upon him. He was brilliant and most daring in his interpretation of the words. He positively alarmed me. He said something like the following: 'Happy medium, indeed. Do you know "happy medium" are two words which mean "miserable mediocrity"? I say, go first class or third; marry a duchess or her kitchenmaid. The happy medium means respectability, and respectability means insipidness. Does it not, Mr Pooter?'

I was so taken aback by being personally appealed to, that I could only bow apologetically, and say I feared I was not competent to offer an opinion. Carrie was about to say something; but she was interrupted, for which I was rather pleased, for she is not clever at argument, and one has to be extra clever to discuss a subject with a man like Mr Huttle.

He continued, with an amazing eloquence that made his unwelcome opinions positively convincing: 'The happy medium is nothing more or less than a vulgar half-measure. A man who loves champagne and, finding a pint too little, fears to face a whole bottle and has recourse to an imperial pint,* will never build a Brooklyn Bridge* or an Eiffel Tower.* No, he is half-hearted, he is a half-measure—respectable—in fact, a happy medium, and will spend the rest of his days in a suburban villa with a stucco-column portico, resembling a four-post bedstead.'

We all laughed.

'That sort of thing,' continued Mr Huttle, 'belongs to a soft man, with a soft beard, with a soft head, with a made tie that hooks on.'

This seemed rather personal and twice I caught myself looking in the glass of the chiffonière; for *I* had on a tie that hooked on—and why not? If these remarks were not personal they were rather careless, and so were some of his subsequent observations, which must have made both Mr Franching and his guests rather uncomfortable. I don't think Mr Huttle meant to be personal, for he added; 'We don't know that class here in this country: but we do in America, and I've no use for them.'

Franching several times suggested that the wine should be passed round the table, which Mr Huttle did not heed; but continued as if he were giving a lecture:

'What we want in America is your homes. We live on wheels. Your simple, quiet life and home, Mr Franching, are charming. No display, no pretension! You make no difference in your dinner, I dare say, when you sit down by yourself and when you invite us. You have your own personal attendant—no hired waiter to breathe on the back of your head.'

I saw Franching palpably wince at this.

Mr Huttle continued: 'Just a small dinner with a few good things, such as you have this evening. You don't insult your guests by sending to the grocer for champagne at six shillings a bottle.'

I could not help thinking of 'Jackson Frères' at three-and-six!

'In fact,' said Mr Huttle, 'a man is little less than a murderer who does. That is the province of the milksop, who wastes his evening at home playing dominoes with his wife. I've heard of these people. We don't want them at this table. Our party is well selected. We've no use for deaf old women, who cannot follow intellectual conversation.'

All our eyes were turned to Mrs Field, who fortunately, being deaf, did not hear his remarks; but continued smiling approval.

'We have no representative at Mr Franching's table,' said Mr Huttle, 'of the unenlightened frivolous matron, who goes to a second-class dance at Bayswater and fancies she is in Society. Society does not know her; it has no use for her.'

Mr Huttle paused for a moment and the opportunity was afforded for the ladies to rise. I asked Mr Franching quietly to excuse me, as I did not wish to miss the last train, which we very nearly did, by-the-by, through Carrie having mislaid the little cloth cricket-cap which she wears when we go out.

It was very late when Carrie and I got home; but on entering the sitting-room I said: 'Carrie, what do you think of Mr Hardfur Huttle?' She simply answered: 'How like Lupin!' The same idea occurred to me in the train. The comparison kept me awake half the night. Mr Huttle was, of course, an older and more influential man; but he *was* like Lupin, and it made me think how dangerous Lupin would be if he were older and more influential. I feel proud to think Lupin *does* resemble Mr Huttle in some ways. Lupin, like Mr Huttle, has original and sometimes wonderful ideas; but it is those ideas that are so dangerous. They make men extremely rich or extremely poor. They make or break men. I always feel people are happier who live a simple unsophisticated life. I believe *I* am happy because I am not ambitious. Somehow I feel that Lupin, since he has been with Mr Perkupp, has become content to settle down and follow the footsteps of his father. This is a comfort.

CHAPTER XXI

Lupin is discharged. We are in great trouble. Lupin gets engaged elsewhere at a handsome salary.

MAY 13.—A terrible misfortune has happened. Lupin is discharged from Mr Perkupp's office, and I scarcely know how I am writing my diary. I was away from office last Sat., the first time I have been absent through illness for twenty years. I believe I was poisoned by some lobster. Mr Perkupp was also absent, as Fate would have it; and our most valued customer, Mr Crowbillon, went to the office in a rage, and withdrew his custom. My boy Lupin not only had the assurance to receive him, but recommended him the firm of Gylterson, Sons and Co. Limited. In my own humble judgement, and though I have to say it against my own son, this seems an act of treachery.

This morning I receive a letter from Perkupp, informing me that Lupin's services are no longer required, and an interview with me is desired at eleven o'clock. I went down to the office with an aching heart, dreading an interview with Mr Perkupp, with whom I have never had a word. I saw nothing of Lupin in the morning. He had not got up when it was time for me to leave, and Carrie said I should do no good by disturbing him. My mind wandered so at the office that I could not do my work properly.

As I expected, I was sent for by Mr Perkupp, and the following conversation ensued as nearly as I can remember it.

Mr Perkupp said: 'Good-morning, Mr Pooter! This is a very serious business. I am not referring so much to the dismissal of your son, for I knew we should have to part sooner or later. *I* am the head of this old, influential, and much-respected firm; and when *I* consider the time has come to revolutionize the business, *I* will do it myself.'

I could see my good master was somewhat affected, and I said: 'I hope, sir, you do not imagine that I have in any way countenanced my son's unwarrantable interference?' Mr Perkupp rose from his seat and took my hand, and said: 'Mr Pooter, I would as soon suspect myself as suspect you.' I was so agitated that in the confusion, to show my gratitude, I very nearly called him a 'grand old man'.

Fortunately I checked myself in time, and said he was a 'grand old master'. I was so unaccountable for my actions that I sat down, leaving him standing. Of course, I at once rose, but Mr Perkupp bade me sit down, which I was very pleased to do. Mr Perkupp, resuming, said: 'You will understand, Mr Pooter, that the high-standing nature of our firm will not admit of our bending to anybody. If Mr Crowbillon chooses to put his work into other hands—I may add, less experienced hands—it is not for us to bend and beg back his custom.' 'You *shall* not do it, sir,' I said with indignation. 'Exactly,' replied Mr Perkupp; 'I shall *not* do it. But I was thinking this, Mr Pooter. Mr Crowbillon is our most valued client, and I will even confess—for I know this will not go beyond ourselves—that we cannot afford very well to lose him, especially in these times, which are not of the brightest. Now, I fancy you can be of service.'

I replied: 'Mr Perkupp, I will work day and night to serve you!'

Mr Perkupp said: 'I know you will. Now, what I should like you to do is this. You yourself might write to Mr Crowbillon—you must not, of course, lead him to suppose I know anything about your doing so—and explain to him that your son was only taken on as a clerk—quite an inexperienced one in fact—out of the respect the firm had for you, Mr Pooter. This is, of course, a fact. I don't suggest that you should speak in too strong terms of your own son's conduct; but I may add, that had he been a son of mine, I should have condemned his interference with no measured terms. That I leave to you. I think the result will be that Mr Crowbillon will see the force of the foolish step he has taken, and our firm will neither suffer in dignity nor in pocket.'

I could not help thinking what a noble gentleman Mr Perkupp is. His manners and his way of speaking seem to almost thrill one with respect.

I said: 'Would you like to see the letter before I send it?'

Mr Perkupp said: 'Oh no! I had better not. I am supposed to know nothing about it, and I have every confidence in you. You must write the letter carefully. We are not very busy; you had better take the morning tomorrow, or the whole day if you like. I shall be here myself all day tomorrow, in fact all the week, in case Mr Crowbillon should call.'

I went home a little more cheerful, but I left word with Sarah that I could not see either Gowing or Cummings, nor in fact anybody, if they called in the evening. Lupin came into the parlour for a moment with a new hat on, and asked my opinion of it. I said I was not in the mood to judge of hats, and I did not think he was in a position to buy a new one. Lupin replied carelessly: 'I didn't buy it; it was a present.'

I have such terrible suspicions of Lupin now that I scarcely like to ask him questions, as I dread the answers so. He, however, saved me the trouble.

He said: 'I met a friend, an old friend, that I did not quite think a friend at the time; but it's all right. As he wisely said, "all is fair in love and war", and there was no reason why we should not be friends still. He's a jolly good, all-round sort of fellow, and a very different stamp from that inflated fool of a Perkupp.'

I said: 'Hush, Lupin! Do not, pray, add insult to injury.'

Lupin said: 'What do you mean by injury? I repeat, I have done no injury. Crowbillon is simply tired of a stagnant stick-in-the-mud firm, and made the change on his own account. I simply recommended the new firm as a matter of biz*—good old biz!'

I said quietly: 'I don't understand your slang, and at my time of life have no desire to learn it; so, Lupin, my boy, let us change the subject. I will, if it please you, *try* and be interested in your new hat adventure.'

Lupin said: 'Oh! there's nothing much about it, except I have not once seen him since his marriage, and he said he was very pleased to see me, and hoped we should be friends. I stood a drink to cement the friendship, and he stood me a new hat—one of his own.'

I said rather wearily: 'But you have not told me your old friend's name?'

Lupin said, with affected carelessness: 'Oh! didn't I? Well, I will. It was *Murray Posh*.'

MAY 14.—Lupin came down late, and seeing me at home all the morning, asked the reason of it. Carrie and I both agreed it was better to say nothing to him about the letter I was writing, so I evaded the question.

Lupin went out, saying he was going to lunch with Murray Posh in the City. I said I hoped Mr Posh would provide him with a berth. Lupin went out laughing, saying: 'I don't mind *wearing* Posh's one-priced hats, but I am not going to *sell* them.' Poor boy, I fear he is perfectly hopeless.

It took me nearly the whole day to write to Mr Crowbillon. Once or twice I asked Carrie for suggestions; and although it seems ungrateful, her suggestions were none of them to the point, while one or two were absolutely idiotic. Of course I did not tell her so. I got the letter off, and took it down to the office for Mr Perkupp to see, but he again repeated that he could trust me.

Gowing called in the evening, and I was obliged to tell him about Lupin and Mr Perkupp; and, to my surprise, he was quite inclined to side with Lupin. Carrie joined in, and said she thought I was taking much too melancholy a view of it. Gowing produced a pint sample-bottle of Madeira, which had been given him, which he said would get rid of the blues. I dare say it would have done so if there had been more of it; but as Gowing helped himself to three glasses, it did not leave much for Carrie and me to get rid of the blues with.

MAY 15.—A day of great anxiety, for I expected every moment a letter from Mr Crowbillon. Two letters came in the evening—one for me, with 'Crowbillon Hall' printed in large gold-and-red letters on the back of the envelope; the other for Lupin, which I felt inclined to open and read, as it had 'Gylterson, Sons, and Co. Limited', which was the recommended firm. I trembled as I opened Mr Crowbillon's letter. I wrote him sixteen pages, closely written; he wrote me less than sixteen lines.

His letter was:

'Sir,
I totally disagree with you. Your son, in the course of five minutes' conversation, displayed more intelligence than your firm has done during the last five years.
Yours faithfully, Gilbert E. Gillam O. Crowbillon.'

What am I to do? Here is a letter that I dare not show to Mr Perkupp, and would not show to Lupin for anything. The crisis had yet to come; for Lupin arrived, and, opening his letter, showed a cheque for £25 as a commission for the recommendation of Mr Crowbillon, whose custom to Mr Perkupp is evidently lost for ever. Cummings and Gowing both called, and both took Lupin's part. Cummings went so far as to say that Lupin would make a name yet. I suppose I was melancholy, for I could only ask: 'Yes, but what sort of a name?'

MAY 16.—I told Mr Perkupp the contents of the letter in a modified form, but Mr Perkupp said: 'Pray don't discuss the matter; it is at an end. Your son will bring his punishment upon himself.' I went home in the evening, thinking of the hopeless future of Lupin. I found him in most extravagant spirits and in evening dress. He threw a letter on the table for me to read.

To my amazement, I read that Gylterson and Sons had absolutely engaged Lupin at a salary of £200 a year, with other advantages. I read the letter through three times and thought it must have been for me. But there it was—Lupin Pooter—plain enough. I was silent. Lupin said: 'What price Perkupp now? You take my tip, Guv.—"off" with Perkupp and freeze on to Gylterson, the firm of the future! Perkupp's firm? The stagnant dummies have been standing still for years, and now are moving back. I want to go *on*. In fact I must go *off*, as I am dining with the Murray Poshes tonight.'

In the exuberance of his spirits he hit his hat with his stick, gave a loud war 'Whoo-oop', jumped over a chair, and took the liberty of rumpling my hair all over my forehead, and bounced out of the room, giving me no chance of reminding him of his age and the respect which was due to his parent. Gowing and Cummings came in the evening, and positively cheered me up with congratulations respecting Lupin.

Gowing said: 'I always said he would get on, and, take my word, he has more in his head than we three put together.'

Carrie said: 'He is a second Hardfur Huttle.'

CHAPTER XXII

Master Percy Edgar Smith James. Mrs James (of Sutton) visits us again and introduces 'Spiritual Séances'.

MAY 26, SUNDAY.—We went to Sutton after dinner to have meat-tea* with Mr and Mrs James. I had no appetite, having dined well at two, and the entire evening was spoiled by little Percy—their only son— who seems to me to be an utterly spoiled child.

Two or three times he came up to me and deliberately kicked my shins. He hurt me once so much that the tears came into my eyes. I gently remonstrated with him, and Mrs James said: 'Please don't scold him; I do not believe in being too severe with young children. You spoil their character.'

Little Percy set up a deafening yell here, and when Carrie tried to pacify him, he slapped her face.

I was so annoyed, I said: 'That is not my idea of bringing up children, Mrs James.'

Mrs James said: 'People have different ideas of bringing up children—even your son Lupin is not the standard of perfection.'

A Mr Mezzini (an Italian, I fancy) here took Percy in his lap. The child wriggled and kicked and broke away from Mr Mezzini, saying: 'I don't like you—you've got a dirty face.'

A very nice gentleman, Mr Birks Spooner, took the child by the wrist and said: 'Come here, dear, and listen to this.'

He detached his chronometer* from the chain and made his watch strike six.

To our horror, the child snatched it from his hand and bounced it down upon the ground like one would a ball.

Mr Birks Spooner was most amiable, and said he could easily get a new glass put in, and did not suppose the works were damaged.

To show you how people's opinions differ, Carrie said the child was bad-tempered, but it made up for that defect by its looks, for it was—in her mind—an unquestionably beautiful child.

I may be wrong, but I do not think I have seen a much uglier child myself. That is *my* opinion.

Master Percy Edgar Smith James

MAY 30.—I don't know why it is, but I never anticipate with any pleasure the visits to our house of Mrs James, of Sutton. She is coming again to stay for a few days. I said to Carrie this morning, as I was leaving: 'I wish, dear Carrie, I could like Mrs James better than I do.'

Carrie said: 'So do I, dear; but as for years I have had to put up with Mr Gowing, who is vulgar, and Mr Cummings, who is kind but most uninteresting, I am sure, dear, you won't mind the occasional visits of Mrs James, who has more intellect in her little finger than both your friends have in their entire bodies.'

I was so entirely taken back by this onslaught on my two dear old friends, I could say nothing, and as I heard the 'bus coming, I left with a hurried kiss—a little too hurried, perhaps, for my upper lip came in contact with Carrie's teeth and slightly cut it. It was quite painful for an hour afterwards. When I came home in the evening I found Carrie buried in a book on Spiritualism, called *There is no Birth*, by Florence

Singleyet.* I need scarcely say the book was sent her to read by Mrs James, of Sutton. As she had not a word to say outside her book, I spent the rest of the evening altering the stair-carpets, which are beginning to show signs of wear at the edges.

Mrs James arrived and, as usual, in the evening took the entire management of everything. Finding that she and Carrie were making some preparations for table-turning,* I thought it time really to put my foot down. I have always had the greatest contempt for such nonsense, and put an end to it years ago when Carrie, at our old house, used to have seances every night with poor Mrs Fussters (who is now dead). If I could see any use in it, I would not care. As I stopped it in the days gone by I determined to do so now.

I said: 'I am very sorry, Mrs James, but I totally disapprove of it, apart from the fact that I receive my old friends on this evening.'

Mrs James said: 'Do you mean to say you haven't read *There is no Birth*?' I said: 'No, and I have no intention of doing so.' Mrs James seemed surprised and said: 'All the world is going mad over the book.' I responded rather cleverly: 'Let it. There will be one sane man in it, at all events.'

Mrs James said she thought it was very unkind, and if people were all as prejudiced as I was, there would never have been the electric telegraph or the telephone.*

I said that was quite a different thing.

Mrs James said sharply: 'In what way, pray—in what way?'

I said: 'In many ways.'

Mrs James said: 'Well, mention *one* way.'

I replied quietly: 'Pardon me, Mrs James; I decline to discuss the matter. I am not interested in it.'

Sarah at this moment opened the door and showed in Cummings, for which I was thankful, for I felt it would put a stop to this foolish table-turning. But I was entirely mistaken; for, on the subject being opened again, Cummings said he was most interested in Spiritualism, although he was bound to confess he did not believe much in it; still, he was willing to be convinced.

I firmly declined to take any part in it, with the result that my presence was ignored. I left the three sitting in the parlour at a small round table which they had taken out of the drawing-room. I walked into the hall with the ultimate intention of taking a little stroll. As I opened the door, who should come in but Gowing!

On hearing what was going on, he proposed that we should join the circle and he would go into a trance. He added that he *knew* a few things about old Cummings, and would *invent* a few about Mrs James. Knowing how dangerous Gowing is, I declined to let him take part in any such foolish performance. Sarah asked me if she could go out for half an hour, and I gave her permission, thinking it would be more comfortable to sit with Gowing in the kitchen than in the cold drawing-room. We talked a good deal about Lupin and Mr and Mrs Murray Posh, with whom he is as usual spending the evening. Gowing said: 'I say, it wouldn't be a bad thing for Lupin if old Posh kicked the bucket.'

My heart gave a leap of horror, and I rebuked Gowing very sternly for joking on such a subject. I lay awake half the night thinking of it—the other half was spent in nightmares on the same subject.

MAY 31.—I wrote a stern letter to the laundress. I was rather pleased with the letter, for I thought it very satirical. I said: 'You have returned the handkerchiefs without the colour. Perhaps you will return either the colour or the value of the handkerchiefs.' I shall be rather curious to know what she will have to say.

More table-turning in the evening. Carrie said last night was in a measure successful, and they ought to sit again. Cummings came in, and seemed interested. I had the gas lighted in the drawing-room, got the steps, and repaired the cornice, which has been a bit of an eyesore to me. In a fit of unthinkingness—if I may use such an expression,—I gave the floor over the parlour, where the seance was taking place, two loud raps with the hammer. I felt sorry afterwards, for it was the sort of ridiculous, foolhardy thing that Gowing or Lupin would have done.

However, they never even referred to it, but Carrie declared that a message came through the table to her of a wonderful description, concerning someone whom she and I knew years ago, and who was quite unknown to the others.

When we went to bed, Carrie asked me as a favour to sit tomorrow night, to oblige her. She said it seemed rather unkind and unsociable on my part. I promised I would sit once.

JUNE 1.—I sat reluctantly at the table in the evening, and I am bound to admit some curious things happened. I contend they were coincidences, but they were curious. For instance, the table kept tilting towards me, which Carrie construed as a desire that I should ask the spirit a question. I obeyed the rules, and I asked the spirit (who said her name was Lina) if she could tell me the name of an old aunt of whom I was thinking, and whom we used to call Aunt Maggie. The table spelled out C A T. We could make nothing out of it, till I suddenly remembered that her second name was Catherine, which it was evidently trying to spell. I don't think even Carrie knew this. But if she did, she would never cheat. I must admit it was curious. Several other things happened, and I consented to sit at another seance on Monday.

JUNE 3.—The laundress called, and said she was very sorry about the handkerchiefs, and returned ninepence. I said, as the colour was completely washed out and the handkerchiefs quite spoiled, ninepence was not enough. Carrie replied that the two handkerchiefs originally only cost sixpence, for she remembered buying them at a sale at the Holloway *Bon Marché*.* In that case, I insisted that threepence should be returned to the laundress. Lupin has gone to stay with the Poshes for a few days. I must say I feel very uncomfortable about it. Carrie said I was ridiculous to worry about it. Mr Posh was very fond of Lupin, who, after all, was only a mere boy.

In the evening we had another seance, which, in some respects, was very remarkable, although the first part of it was a little doubtful. Gowing called, as well as Cummings, and begged to be allowed to join the circle. I wanted to object, but Mrs James, who appears a good Medium (that is, if there is anything in it at all), thought there might be a little more spirit power if Gowing joined; so the five of us sat down.

The moment I turned out the gas, and almost before I could get my hands on the table, it rocked violently and tilted, and began moving quickly across the room. Gowing shouted out: 'Way, oh! steady, lad, steady!' I told Gowing if he could not behave himself I should light the gas, and put an end to the seance. To tell the truth, I thought Gowing was playing tricks, and I hinted as much; but Mrs James said she had often seen the table go right off the ground. The spirit Lina came again, and said, 'WARN' three or four times, and declined to explain. Mrs James said 'Lina' was stubborn sometimes. She often behaved like that, and the best thing to do was to send her away.

She then hit the table sharply, and said: 'Go away, Lina; you are disagreeable. Go away!' I should think we sat nearly three-quarters of an hour with nothing happening. My hands felt quite cold, and I suggested we should stop the seance. Carrie and Mrs James, as well as Cummings, would not agree to it. In about ten minutes' time there was some tilting towards me. I gave the alphabet, and it spelled out SPOOF. As I have heard both Gowing and Lupin use the word, and as I could hear Gowing silently laughing, I directly accused him of pushing the table. He denied it; but, I regret to say, I did not believe him.

Gowing said: 'Perhaps it means "Spook", a ghost.'

I said: '*You* know it doesn't mean anything of the sort.'

Gowing said: 'Oh! very well—I'm sorry I "spook",' and he rose from the table.

No one took any notice of the stupid joke, and Mrs James suggested he should sit out for a while. Gowing consented and sat in the armchair.

The table began to move again, and we might have had a wonderful seance but for Gowing's stupid interruptions. In answer to the alphabet from Carrie the table spelt 'NIPUL', then the 'WARN' three times. We could not think what it meant till Cummings pointed out that 'NIPUL' was Lupin spelled backwards. This was quite exciting. Carrie was particularly excited, and said she hoped nothing horrible was going to happen.

Mrs James asked if 'Lina' was the spirit. The table replied firmly, 'No', and the spirit would not give his or her name. We then had the message, 'NIPUL will be very rich.'

Carrie said she felt quite relieved, but the word 'WARN' was again spelt out. The table then began to oscillate violently, and in reply to Mrs James, who spoke very softly to the table, the spirit began to spell its name. It first spelled 'DRINK'.

Gowing here said: 'Ah! that's more in my line.'

I asked him to be quiet as the name might not be completed.

The table then spelt 'WATER'.

Gowing here interrupted again, and said: 'Ah! that's *not* in my line. *Outside* if you like, but not inside.'

Carrie appealed to him to be quiet.

The table then spelt 'CAPTAIN', and Mrs James startled us by crying out, 'Captain Drinkwater, a very old friend of my father's, who has been dead some years.'

This was more interesting, and I could not help thinking that after all there must be something in Spiritualism.

Mrs James asked the spirit to interpret the meaning of the word 'Warn' as applied to 'NIPUL'. The alphabet was given again, and we got the word 'BOSH'.

Gowing here muttered: 'So it is.'

Mrs James said she did not think the spirit meant that, as Captain Drinkwater was a perfect gentleman, and would never have used the word in answer to a lady's question. Accordingly the alphabet was given again.

This time the table spelled distinctly 'POSH'. We all thought of Mrs Murray Posh and Lupin. Carrie was getting a little distressed, and as it was getting late we broke up the circle.

We arranged to have one more tomorrow, as it will be Mrs James' last night in town. We also determined *not* to have Gowing present.

Cummings, before leaving, said it was certainly interesting, but he wished the spirits would say something about him.

JUNE 4.—Quite looking forward to the seance this evening. Was thinking of it all the day at the office.

Just as we sat down at the table we were annoyed by Gowing entering without knocking.

He said: 'I am not going to stop, but I have brought with me a sealed envelope, which I know I can trust with Mrs Pooter. In that sealed envelope is a strip of paper on which I have asked a simple question. If the spirits can answer that question, I will believe in Spiritualism.'

I ventured the expression that it might be impossible.

Mrs James said: 'Oh no! it is of common occurrence for the spirits to answer questions under such conditions—and even for them to write on locked slates. It is quite worth trying. If "Lina" is in a good temper, she is certain to do it.'

Gowing said: 'All right; then I shall be a firm believer. I shall perhaps drop in about half-past nine or ten, and hear the result.'

He then left and we sat a long time. Cummings wanted to know something about some undertaking in which he was concerned, but he could get no answer of any description whatever—at which he said he was very disappointed and was afraid there was not much in table-turning after all. I thought this rather selfish of him. The seance was very similar to the one last night, almost the same in fact. So we turned to the letter. 'Lina' took a long time answering the question, but eventually spelt out 'ROSES, LILIES, AND COWS'. There was great rocking of the table at this time, and Mrs James said: 'If that is Captain Drinkwater, let us ask him the answer as well?'

It was the spirit of the Captain, and, most singular, he gave the same identical answer: 'ROSES, LILIES, AND COWS.'

I cannot describe the agitation with which Carrie broke the seal, or the disappointment we felt on reading the question, to which the answer was so inappropriate. The question was, *'What's old Pooter's age?'*

This quite decided me.

As I had put my foot down on Spiritualism years ago, so I would again.

I am pretty easy-going as a rule, but I can be extremely firm when driven to it.

I said slowly, as I turned up the gas: 'This is the last of this nonsense that shall ever take place under my roof. I regret I permitted myself to be a party to such tomfoolery. If there is anything in it—which I doubt—it is nothing of any good, and I *won't have it again*. That is enough.'

Mrs James said: 'I think, Mr Pooter, you are rather over-stepping——'

I said: 'Hush, madam. I am master of this house—please understand that.'

Mrs James made an observation which I sincerely hope I was mistaken in. I was in such a rage I could not quite catch what she said. But if I thought she said what it sounded like, she should never enter the house again.

CHAPTER XXIII

Lupin leaves us. We dine at his new apartments, and hear some extraordinary information respecting the wealth of Mr Murray Posh. Meet Miss Lilian Posh. Am sent for by Mr Hardfur Huttle. Important.

JULY 1.—I find, on looking over my diary, nothing of any consequence has taken place during the last month. Today we lose Lupin, who has taken furnished apartments at Bayswater, near his friends, Mr and Mrs Murray Posh, at two guineas a week. I think this is most extravagant of him, as it is half his salary. Lupin says one never loses by a good address, and, to use his own expression, Brickfield Terrace is a bit 'off'.* Whether he means it is 'far off' I do not know. I have long since given up trying to understand his curious expressions. I said the neighbourhood had always been good enough for his parents. His reply was: 'It is no question of being good or bad. There is no money in it, and I am not going to rot away my life in the suburbs.'

We are sorry to lose him, but perhaps he will get on better by himself, and there may be some truth in his remark that an old and a young horse can't pull together in the same cart.

Gowing called, and said that the house seemed quite peaceful, and like old times. He liked Master Lupin very well, but he occasionally suffered from what he could not help—youth.

JULY 2.—Cummings called, looked very pale, and said he had been very ill again, and of course not a single friend had been near him. Carrie said she had never heard of it, whereupon he threw down a copy of the *Bicycle News* on the table, with the following paragraph: 'We regret to hear that that favourite old roadster, Mr Cummings ("Long" Cummings), has met with what might have been a serious accident in Rye Lane. A mischievous boy threw a stick between the spokes of one of the back wheels, and the machine overturned, bringing our brother tricyclist heavily to the ground. Fortunately he was more frightened than hurt, but we missed his merry face at the dinner at Chingford, where they turned up in good numbers. "Long" Cummings' health was proposed by our popular Vice, Mr Westropp, the prince of bicyclists, who in his happiest vein said it was a case of *"Cumming*(s) thro' the *Rye*, but fortunately there was more *wheel* than *woe*," a joke which created roars of laughter.'

We all said we were very sorry, and pressed Cummings to stay to supper. Cummings said it was like old times being without Lupin, and he was much better away.

JULY 3, SUNDAY.—In the afternoon, as I was looking out of the parlour window, which was open, a grand trap, driven by a lady, with a gentleman seated by the side of her, stopped at our door. Not wishing to be seen, I withdrew my head very quickly, knocking the back of it violently against the sharp edge of the window-sash. I was nearly stunned. There was a loud double-knock at the front door; Carrie rushed out of the parlour, upstairs to her room, and I followed, as Carrie thought it was Mr Perkupp. I thought it was Mr Franching. I whispered to Sarah over the banisters: 'Show them into the drawing-room.' Sarah said, as the shutters were not opened, the room would smell musty. There was another loud rat-tat. I whispered: 'Then show them into the parlour, and say Mr Pooter will be down directly.' I changed my coat, but could not see to do my hair, as Carrie was occupying the glass.

Sarah came up, and said it was Mrs Murray Posh and Mr Lupin.

This was quite a relief. I went down with Carrie, and Lupin met me with the remark: 'I say, what did you run away from the window for? Did we frighten you?'

I foolishly said: 'What window?'

Lupin said: 'Oh, you know. Shut it. You looked as if you were playing at Punch and Judy.'

On Carrie asking if she could offer them anything, Lupin said: 'Oh, I think Daisy will take on a cup of tea. I can do with a B. and S.'*

I said: 'I am afraid we have no soda.'

Lupin said: 'Don't bother about that. You just trip out and hold the horse; I don't think Sarah understands it.'

They stayed a very short time, and as they were leaving, Lupin said: 'I want you both to come and dine with me next Wednesday, and see my new place. Mr and Mrs Murray Posh, Miss Posh (Murray's sister) are coming. Eight o'clock sharp. No one else.'

I said we did not pretend to be fashionable people, and would like the dinner earlier, as it made it so late before we got home.

Lupin said: 'Rats! You must get used to it. If it comes to that, Daisy and I can drive you home.'

We promised to go; but I must say in my simple mind the familiar way in which Mrs Posh and Lupin addressed each other is reprehensible. Anybody would think they had been children together. I certainly should object to six months' acquaintance calling *my* wife 'Carrie', and driving out with her.

JULY 4.—Lupin's rooms looked very nice; but the dinner was, I thought, a little too grand, especially as he commenced with champagne straight off. I also think Lupin might have told us that he and Mr and Mrs Murray Posh and Miss Posh were going to put on full evening dress. Knowing that the dinner was only for us six, we never dreamed it would be a full dress affair. I had no appetite. It was quite twenty minutes past eight before we sat down to dinner. At six I could have eaten a hearty meal. I had a bit of bread-and-butter at that hour, feeling famished, and I expect that partly spoiled my appetite.

We were introduced to Miss Posh, whom Lupin called 'Lillie Girl', as if he had known her all his life. She was very tall, rather plain, and I thought she was a little painted round the eyes. I hope I am wrong; but she had such fair hair, and yet her eyebrows were black. She looked about thirty. I did not like the way she kept giggling and giving Lupin smacks and pinching him. Then her laugh was a sort of a scream that went right through my ears, all the more irritating because there was nothing to laugh at. In fact, Carrie and I were not at all prepossessed with her. They all smoked cigarettes after dinner, including Miss Posh, who startled Carrie by saying: 'Don't you smoke, dear?' I answered for Carrie, and said: 'Mrs Charles Pooter has not arrived at it yet,' whereupon Miss Posh gave one of her piercing laughs again.

Mrs Posh sang a dozen songs at least, and I can only repeat what I have said before—she does *not* sing in tune; but Lupin sat by the side of the piano, gazing into her eyes the whole time. If I had been Mr Posh, I think I should have had something to say about it. Mr Posh

'Lillie Girl.'

made himself very agreeable to us, and eventually sent us home in his carriage, which I thought most kind. He is evidently very rich, for Mrs Posh had on some beautiful jewellery. She told Carrie her necklace, which her husband gave her as a birthday present, alone cost £300.

Mr Posh said he had a great belief in Lupin, and thought he would make rapid way in the world.

I could not help thinking of the £600 Mr Posh lost over the Parachikka Chlorates through Lupin's advice.

During the evening I had an opportunity to speak to Lupin, and expressed a hope that Mr Posh was not living beyond his means.

Lupin sneered, and said Mr Posh was worth thousands. 'Posh's one-price hat' was a household word in Birmingham, Manchester,

Liverpool, and all the big towns throughout England. Lupin further informed me that Mr Posh was opening branch establishments at New York, Sydney, and Melbourne, and was negotiating for Kimberley and Johannesburg.

I said I was pleased to hear it.

Lupin said: 'Why, he has settled over £10,000 on Daisy, and the same amount on "Lillie Girl". If at any time I wanted a little capital, he would put up a couple of "thou" at a day's notice, and could buy up Perkupp's firm over his head at any moment with ready cash.'

On the way home in the carriage, for the first time in my life, I was inclined to indulge in the radical thought that money was *not* properly divided.

On arriving home at a quarter-past eleven, we found a hansom cab, which had been waiting for me for two hours with a letter. Sarah said she did not know what to do, as we had not left the address where we had gone. I trembled as I opened the letter, fearing it was some bad news about Mr Perkupp. The note was: 'Dear Mr Pooter, Come down to the Victoria Hotel without delay. Important. Yours truly, Hardfur Huttle.'

I asked the cabman if it was too late. The cabman replied that it was *not*; for his instructions were, if I happened to be out, he was to wait till I came home. I felt very tired, and really wanted to go to bed. I reached the hotel at a quarter before midnight. I apologized for being so late, but Mr Huttle said: 'Not at all; come and have a few oysters.' I feel my heart beating as I write these words. To be brief, Mr Huttle said he had a rich American friend who wanted to do something large in our line of business, and that Mr Franching had mentioned my name to him. We talked over the matter. If, by any happy chance, the result be successful, I can more than compensate my dear master for the loss of Mr Crowbillon's custom. Mr Huttle had previously said: 'The glorious "Fourth"* is a lucky day for America, and, as it has not yet struck twelve, we will celebrate it with a glass of the best wine to be had in the place, and drink good luck to our bit of business.'

I fervently hope it will bring good luck to us all.

It was two o'clock when I got home. Although I was so tired, I could not sleep except for short intervals—then only to dream.

I kept dreaming of Mr Perkupp and Mr Huttle. The latter was in a lovely palace with a crown on. Mr Perkupp was waiting in the room. Mr Huttle kept taking off this crown and handing it to me, and calling me 'President'.

He appeared to take no notice of Mr Perkupp, and I kept asking Mr Huttle to give the crown to my worthy master. Mr Huttle kept saying: 'No, this is the White House of Washington, and you must keep your crown, Mr President.'

We all laughed long and very loudly, till I got parched, and then I woke up. I fell asleep, only to dream the same thing over and over again.

CHAPTER THE LAST

One of the happiest days of my life.

JULY 10.—The excitement and anxiety through which I have gone the last few days have been almost enough to turn my hair grey. It is all but settled. Tomorrow the die will be cast. I have written a long letter to Lupin—feeling it my duty to do so—regarding his attention to Mrs Posh, for they drove up to our house again last night.

JULY 11.—I find my eyes filling with tears as I open the note of my interview this morning with Mr Perkupp. Addressing me, he said: 'My faithful servant, I will not dwell on the important service you have done our firm. You can never be sufficiently thanked. Let us change the subject. Do you like your house, and are you happy where you are?'

I replied: 'Yes, sir; I love my house and I love the neighbourhood, and could not bear to leave it.'

Mr Perkupp, to my surprise, said: 'Mr Pooter, I will purchase the freehold of that house, and present it to the most honest and most worthy man it has ever been my lot to meet.'

He shook my hand, and said he hoped my wife and I would be spared many years to enjoy it. My heart was too full to thank him; and, seeing my embarrassment, the good fellow said: 'You need say nothing, Mr Pooter,' and left the office.

I sent telegrams to Carrie, Gowing, and Cummings (a thing I have never done before), and asked the two latter to come round to supper.

On arriving home I found Carrie crying with joy, and I sent Sarah round to the grocer's to get two bottles of 'Jackson Frères'.

My two dear friends came in the evening, and the last post brought a letter from Lupin in reply to mine. I read it aloud to them all. It ran: 'My dear old Guv., Keep your hair on. You are on the wrong tack again. I am engaged to be married to "Lillie Girl". I did not mention it last Thursday, as it was not definitely settled. We shall be married in August, and amongst our guests we hope to see your old friends Gowing and Cummings. With much love to all, from *The same old Lupin.*'

THE END

EXPLANATORY NOTES

3 *'The Laurels'*: C. F. G. Masterman, in *The Condition of England* (1909), cites as typical suburban housenames 'Homelea', 'Belle View', 'Buona Vista', 'Sunnyhurst', and 'The Laurels' (p. 89).

Holloway: area of North London, on the borders between true suburbia and the inner city.

'Sylvia Gavotte': by the late nineteenth century the gavotte was considered an 'old-fashioned' dance, albeit one executed to a 'lively' and 'dainty' rhythm: Mrs Lilly Grove, *Dancing* (London: Longmans, Green & Co., 1895).

Collard and Collard: sellers of musical instruments, with showrooms at 16 Grosvenor Street and two other branches.

4 *meerschaum*: pipe made out of sepiolite, a white clay-like substance.

8 *carmine*: red or crimson pigment obtained from cochineal.

9 *the quarter-to-nine 'bus to the city*: the 'Favourite', a dark green bus, ran the route from the Holloway Road via the Angel, Gray's Inn Road, Chancery Lane, Strand, Whitehall, and Victoria Street, to Victoria.

10 *green cigar*: made of tobacco leaves which had not been dried.

green rep: fabric with a corded surface (the *OED* dates it to 1883).

11 *Blackheath*: area of south-east London, with village, heath and much building of quality villas in the late nineteenth century.

15 *Kinahan*: brand of Irish whiskey, manufactured in Dublin.

18 *Sutton*: to the south of London, gradually becoming incorporated within the suburban radius.

Italian Opera, Haymarket, Savoy, or Lyceum: Her Majesty's Theatre; the Theatre Royal, Haymarket, first opened in 1720, was rebuilt in 1880, and came under Beerbohm Tree's management in 1887; the Savoy opened in 1881 for the performance of Gilbert and Sullivan's comic operas; the Lyceum, in Wellington Street, off the Strand, constructed in 1834, was noted for 'Shakespearean drama, melodrama, and romantic plays (Mr. Henry Irving and Miss Ellen Terry)' (*Black's Guide to London and its Environs*, 9th edn. London: Adam & Charles Black, 1891, 86).

Tank Theatre, Islington: the most likely model for this is the Grand Theatre, Islington, which opened in 1870 as the Philharmonic Theatre, burned down in 1882 and again in 1887, and was reopened on 4 August 1888 as the Grand.

'Angel': the Angel, Islington: area around the road junction on the fringes of inner North London.

19 *Bézique*: card game for two players, introduced to England in 1861, in which the name 'Bézique' is applied to the occurrence in one hand of the Knave of Diamonds and the Queen of Spades.

20 *Bicycle News*: the British Union Catalogue of Periodicals reveals the prime decade for the emergence of bicycling journals to have been the 1870s. The progress of the craze—and the fact that there is something a little dated about Cumming's enthusiasm—is suggested by the fact that *Bicycling News*, launched in 1876, was in 1886 absorbed into *Sport and Play*.

21 *half-a-sovereign*: ten shillings and sixpence, or about 53 pence in today's coinage.

22 *Marat*: Jean-Paul Marat, 1743–93, French politician, physician, journalist, and leading radical in the French Revolution, had to take frequent baths to soothe a skin condition: during one of these he was assassinated by Charlotte Corday.

Madame Tussaud's: London exhibition of wax models of pre-eminent and notorious people, established by Madame Tussaud in 1802.

24 *Mansion House*: the official residence of the Lord Mayor of London, first used 1753.

26 *chimney-glass*: looking-glass commonly placed over the mantelpiece.

Kachu eagle: the Kachu is a mountain range in the eastern Caucasus.

Shoolbred's: store situated at 150 Tottenham Court Road.

28 *lodge*: the place of meeting for members of a branch of freemasons, or the meeting of such a branch.

30 *M.L.L.*: an obscure Masonic abbreviation, signifying Maître des Loges Légitimes (see *Kenning's Masonic Cyclopaedia*, ed. Revd. F. A. Woodford, London: George Kenning, 1878).

34 *'consequences'*: parlour game, in which each person playing writes an element of a sequence: 1. an adjective; 2. the name of a man; 3. whom the man met (this must be a woman); 4. where they met; 5. what he gave her; 6. what he said to her; 7. what she replied; 8. what the consequence was; 9. what the world said. The paper is folded after each line and passed on to one's neighbour, who continues the process until completion involves the unfolding of the papers and the reading out of the incongruous narratives.

'The Garden of Sleep': by Isidore de Lara, words by Clement Scott. The garden in question is a graveyard.

Mr Gladstone: William Ewart Gladstone (1809–98), Liberal politician and Prime Minister.

36 *views of Japan*: a variety of Japanese manufactured goods were shown at

the International Exhibition in London in 1862, and a 'Japanese mania' in interior decoration and aesthetic taste began towards the middle of the following year. By 1885, James McNeill Whistler, who had been much influenced by Japanese style, was complaining, in his 'Ten O'Clock' lecture, against the thoughtless appropriation of Oriental motifs.

38 *Garibaldi*: a kind of blouse, originally bright red, in imitation of the shirt worn by Garibaldi's Italian followers; later made in other colours.

Exchange and Mart: a weekly publication of small advertisements. From 1871 to 1928 its full title was *Bazaar, Exchange and Mart*.

39 *the helmet worn in India*: the topi.

42 *got the chuck!*: to have been sacked (the *OED* cites this source to date the phrase).

44 *'Cutlets'*: Patrick Beaver, in *Victorian Party Games* (London: Peter Davis, 1974, 53), describes this as a variant of 'Quakers' Meeting', which he explains thus: 'The company arrange themselves on the floor in a straight line, all kneeling on the right knee while on the other knee they rest their hands and twiddle their thumbs. It is forbidden to smile—any player detected doing so having to pay a forfeit. The following conversation is then carried on, each line of which must be repeated in turn by every player before the next line is said.

Well friend, and how art thou?
Hast thou heard of Brother Obadiah's death?
No, how did he die?
With one finger up (As each player repeats this line he stops twisting his thumbs and holds up his right forefinger),
With one eye shut (Each closes his right eye),
And shoulder all awry (Each does this).
How did he die?
In this way.

'At this point the player at the top of the row gives his neighbour a mighty shove and the whole company goes over like a pack of cards.'

47 *dog-carts*: an open vehicle for ordinary driving, with two transverse seats back to back.

49 *'Muggings'*: or Muggins; a simple card-game, very like Snap.

51 *'Is Marriage a Failure?'*: series of letters appearing in the *Daily Telegraph* during the summer of 1888. These were lampooned several times in *Punch*: see the spoof letters on the subject (25 August 1888, p. 87); 'Is Smoking a Failure?' (1 September 1888, p. 108); 'Is Detection a Failure?' (20 October 1888, p. 183).

58 *Paysandu tongue*: a quality brand of tinned tongue.

61 *'Some Day'*: the most popular song by Milton Wellings, contemporary

of Arthur Sullivan (see Harold Simpson, *A Century of Ballads, 1810–1910*, London: Mills & Boon, 1910).

62 *Blondin*: pseudonym of Jean-François Gravelet, 1824–97, tightrope walker.

63 *Baldwin's balloon*: Thomas Scott Baldwin, US proprietor of non-rigid airships and hot-air balloooons.

66 *Mr Burwin-Fosselton*: Weedon Grossmith is said to have based his drawings of Burwin-Fosselton on Tom Heslewood, a close friend and a costume-designer.

Mr Irving: Henry Irving (John Henry Brodribb, 1838–1905), actor, lessee, and manager of the Lyceum from 1878, famous for his acting partnership with Ellen Terry. Both the Grossmith brothers imitated Irving: 'Mr Henry Irving and his Leetle Dog' often featured in George's entertainments, including the one he gave before Queen Victoria; Weedon's parody was developed for private amusement.

68 *Mr Hare*: John Hare (John Fairs, 1844–1921), actor-manager of the Garrick Theatre from 1889-1895 and recognized as the greatest character actor of his day, specializing in old men's parts.

71 *Ellen Terry*: 1847–1928, extremely popular actress in Britain and North America.

73 *dandy horse*: an early form of bicycle, in which the rider sat on a bar between the two wheels and propelled himself along by pushing the ground with each foot alternately.

verb. sap.: *verbum sapienti sat est* (Latin); a word to the wise is enough, i.e. a hint is enough to any intelligent person.

Revenons à nos moutons: (French) literally, 'Let us return to our sheep', i.e. let's get back to the subject, originally taken from the comedy *La Farce de Maistre Pathelin*, *c.*1460, and much used by Rabelais.

chacun à son gout: (French) everyone to his own taste.

Vici!: Latin: I have conquered.

the hump-backed Richard: Richard III. Irving played Shakespeare's role in 1877.

74 *Vale!*: Latin: farewell.

75 *Michaelmas Term*: autumn term, called after the quarter-day, when rents were due, which fell on 29 September, the Festival of St Michael and All Angels.

76 *Evelyn and Pepys*: John Evelyn (1620–1706) and Samuel Pepys (1633–1703), famous diarists.

thirteen at dinner: thought to be unlucky. This superstition is said to arise from a banquet in Valhalla (in Norse legend), where Loki was included, making thirteen, and Balder was slain: the superstition seemed confirmed in Christian countries by the Last Supper of Christ and the twelve apostles.

79 *sloppy*: very wet and splashy; covered with water or thin mud.

80 *Lowther Arcade*: off Piccadilly, in central London.

Stradivarius: much prized violin, made by Antonio Stradivarius (1644–1737), of Cremona.

81 *tee-to-tums*: spinning tops.

83 *"outside-halfpenny-'bus-ness"*: it was cheaper (halfpence) to travel on the open top of a horse-drawn omnibus than inside (one penny).

85 *Peter Robinson's*: large department store at 334 Oxford Street.

Consols: Government security without a maturity date. The word is a contraction of Consolidated Annuities. They originated in 1751: the first issue carried an interest rate of 3 per cent, which was reduced to 2¾ per cent in 1888.

Joe Miller: Joseph Miller, 1684–1738: English comedian, and a collection of jests known as *Joe Miller's Jests* appeared in 1739. Subsequently, any stale joke became known as a 'Joe Miller' since it was supposed to emanate from this source.

Financial News: started as the *Financial and Mining News* in January 1884, becoming the *Financial News* in July the same year.

86 *Chlorates*: chemical compounds, especially potassium chlorate, used as a source of elemental oxygen, usually in explosives.

88 *Irving in 'Macbeth'*: a very topical reference, since Irving played Macbeth in early 1889. See *Punch* 5 January 1889, 2: 'An old stager, *laudator temporis Macreadi*, remarked that HENRY IRVING did not possess the physique necessary for the part of *Macbeth*. "He has SHAKESPEARE's authority for doing without it," was Somebody's reply; "for doesn't he make *Macbeth* himself exclaim, 'Throw physique to the dogs, I'll none of it'"." See also *Punch*'s review of the production, 12 January 1889, 15.

90 *marking a half-dozen new collars*: placing an identifying mark on household linen which will be sent out to a laundry by embroidery or stitching, or, more likely here, with indelible marking-ink.

91 *box-coat*: a heavy overcoat worn by coachmen on the box, or by those riding outside on a coach.

93 *hansom cab*: a low-hung two-wheeled cabriolet holding two people inside, driver mounted on an elevated seat behind, and the reins going over the top.

96 *cushion of bacon*: 'the fleshy part of the buttock' (*OED*).

100 *stylographic pen*: a type of pen invented *c.*1880 having no nib, but a fine perforated writing point fed with ink from a reservoir in the stem. A fine

needle is fitted into this point, which when pushed back in the act of writing opens a valve which will permit the flow of ink.

101 *Worcester sauce*: a sharp, spicy bottled condiment.

bounders' ball: a bounder is a person of objectionable manners or anti-social behaviour, but the term is used as a wider term of abuse signifying a bit of a rogue or a cad. The *OED* has 1889 as its first use.

108 *'Simpz'*: probably William Simpson (1823–99), painter of topographical and architectural subjects and illustrator for the *Illustrated London News*, who executed many pictures of India and the Middle East.

109 *Job's comforter*: someone who means to sympathize with one in one's grief but who, in claiming that you brought it upon yourself, makes your sorrow worse. The allusion is to the rebukes which Job received from his 'comforters' in the book named after him in the Old Testament.

111 *Peckham*: area of South London.

113 *Columbus and Stephenson*: Christopher Columbus, *c*.1446–1506, travelled to America in 1492 and 1493; George Stephenson, 1781–1848, perfecter of the locomotive; engineer of the Stockton and Darlington Railway, which, opening 27 September 1825, was the first to carry passengers and goods by steam locomotive.

imperial pint: nationally accepted measure appointed by statute.

Brooklyn Bridge: designed by John Augustus Roebling and largely built by his son, Colonel Washington Roebling, between 1869 and 1883. It is 1,595 feet long, and spans the East River from Brooklyn to Manhattan Island, New Jersey.

Eiffel Tower: the controversial 984-foot wrought-iron structure in Paris was built by the engineer Alexandre-Gustave Eiffel, having been commissioned by the organizers of the 1889 Centennial Exhibition held to commemorate the French Revolution.

118 *biz*: colloquial abbreviation of 'business', American in origin.

121 *meat-tea*: high-tea, eaten in the early evening, and usually consisting of cold meats and/or tinned salmon, salad, bread and butter, and cake.

chronometer: instrument for measuring time, especially applied to time-keepers which have been adjusted to ensure accuracy in all variations of temperature.

123 *There is no Birth, by Florence Singleyet*: George Grossmith's former theatrical companion, Florence Marryat, published a spiritualist work, *There is no Death*, in 1891.

table-turning: in *A Society Clown* (p. 86), George Grossmith records that he once took part in a table-rapping session with Florence Marryat, who accused him of disrespect.

the electric telegraph or the telephone: the 'galvanic' or electric telegraph was invented by 1840; the 'Electrical Speaking Telephone' was introduced by Alexander Graham Bell in 1876.

125 *the Holloway 'Bon Marché'*: department store, named after the more famous Parisian emporium of the same name.

129 *'off'*: socially unacceptable (an earlier usage in this context than is chronicled in the *OED*).

130 *B. and S.*: brandy and soda.

133 *The glorious 'Fourth'*: the Fourth of July: the Declaration of Independence, asserting the sovereign independence of the former British colony, was adopted in America on this date in 1776.

A SELECTION OF   OXFORD WORLD'S CLASSICS

JANE AUSTEN	**Emma** **Persuasion** **Pride and Prejudice** **Sense and Sensibility**
MRS BEETON	**Book of Household Management**
ANNE BRONTË	**The Tenant of Wildfell Hall**
CHARLOTTE BRONTË	**Jane Eyre**
EMILY BRONTË	**Wuthering Heights**
WILKIE COLLINS	**The Moonstone** **The Woman in White**
JOSEPH CONRAD	**Heart of Darkness and Other Tales** **Nostromo**
CHARLES DARWIN	**The Origin of Species**
CHARLES DICKENS	**Bleak House** **David Copperfield** **Great Expectations** **Hard Times**
GEORGE ELIOT	**Middlemarch** **The Mill on the Floss**
ELIZABETH GASKELL	**Cranford**
THOMAS HARDY	**Jude the Obscure** **Tess of the d'Urbervilles**
WALTER SCOTT	**Ivanhoe**
MARY SHELLEY	**Frankenstein**
ROBERT LOUIS STEVENSON	**Treasure Island**
BRAM STOKER	**Dracula**
WILLIAM MAKEPEACE THACKERAY	**Vanity Fair**
OSCAR WILDE	**The Picture of Dorian Gray**

American Literature

British and Irish Literature

Children's Literature

Classics and Ancient Literature

Colonial Literature

Eastern Literature

European Literature

Gothic Literature

History

Medieval Literature

Oxford English Drama

Poetry

Philosophy

Politics

Religion

The Oxford Shakespeare

A complete list of Oxford World's Classics, including Authors in Context, Oxford English Drama, and the Oxford Shakespeare, is available in the UK from the Marketing Services Department, Oxford University Press, Great Clarendon Street, Oxford OX2 6DP, or visit the website at www.oup.com/uk/worldsclassics.

In the USA, visit www.oup.com/us/owc for a complete title list.

Oxford World's Classics are available from all good bookshops. In case of difficulty, customers in the UK should contact Oxford University Press Bookshop, 116 High Street, Oxford OX1 4BR.